Rowdy of the Cross L

B. M. Bower

Alpha Editions

This edition published in 2023

ISBN : 9789357941037

Design and Setting By
Alpha Editions
www.alphaedis.com
Email - info@alphaedis.com

Contents

CHAPTER 1. Lost in a Blizzard.................................- 1 -

CHAPTER 2. Miss Conroy Refuses Shelter....................- 7 -

CHAPTER 3. Rowdy Hires a New Boss.....................- 13 -

CHAPTER 4. Pink as "Chappyrone."......................- 18 -

CHAPTER 5. At Home at Cross L.........................- 23 -

CHAPTER 6. A Shot From the Dark........................- 26 -

CHAPTER 7. Rowdy in a Tough Place.....................- 32 -

CHAPTER 8. Pink in a Threatening Mood. ....- 37 -

CHAPTER 9. Moving the Herd............................- 40 -

CHAPTER 10. Harry Conroy at Home. ....- 44 -

CHAPTER 11. Rowdy Promoted. ....- 48 -

CHAPTER 12. "You Can Tell Jessie."....................- 52 -

CHAPTER 13. Rowdy Finds Happiness. ....- 58 -

CHAPTER 1.
Lost in a Blizzard.

"Rowdy" Vaughan—he had been christened Rowland by his mother, and rechristened Rowdy by his cowboy friends, who are prone to treat with much irreverence the names bestowed by mothers—was not happy. He stood in the stirrups and shook off the thick layer of snow which clung, damp and close-packed, to his coat. The dull yellow folds were full of it; his gray hat, pulled low over his purple ears, was heaped with it. He reached up a gloved hand and scraped away as much as he could, wrapped the long-skirted, "sour-dough" coat around his numbed legs, then settled into the saddle with a shiver of distaste at the plight he was in, and wished himself back at the Horseshoe Bar.

Dixie, standing knee-deep in a drift, shook himself much after the manner of his master; perhaps he, also, wished himself back at the Horseshoe Bar. He turned his head to look back, blinking at the snow which beat insistently in his eyes; he could not hold them open long enough to see anything, however, so he twitched his ears pettishly and gave over the attempt.

"It's up to you, old boy," Rowdy told him resignedly. "I'm plumb lost; I never was in this damn country before, anyhow—and I sure wish I wasn't here now. If you've any idea where we're at, I'm dead willing to have you pilot the layout. Never mind Chub; locating his feed when it's stuck under his nose is his limit."

Chub lifted an ear dispiritedly when his name was spoken; but, as was usually the case, he heard no good of himself, and dropped his head again. No one took heed of him; no one ever did. His part was to carry Vaughan's bed, and to follow unquestionably where Vaughan and Dixie might lead. He was cold and tired and hungry, but his faith in his master was strong; the responsibility of finding shelter before the dark came down rested not with him.

Vaughan pressed his chilled knees against Dixie's ribs, but the hand upon the reins was carefully non-committal; so that Dixie, having no suggestion of his master's wish, ventured to indulge his own. He turned tail squarely to the storm and went straight ahead. Vaughan put his hands deep into his pockets, snuggled farther down into the sheepskin collar of his coat, and rode passive, enduring.

They brought up against a wire fence, and Vaughan, rousing from his apathy, tried to peer through the white, shifting wall of the storm. "You're a swell guide—not," he remarked to the horse. "Now you, you hike down this fence till you locate a gate or a corner, or any darned thing; and I don't give a cuss if the snow does get in your eyes. It's your own fault."

Dixie, sneezing the snow from his nostrils, turned obediently; Chub, his feet dragging wearily in the snow, trailed patiently behind. Half an hour of this, and it seemed as if it would go on forever.

Through the swirl Vaughan could see the posts standing forlornly in the snow, with sixteen feet of blizzard between; at no time could he distinguish more than two or three at once, and there were long minutes when the wall stood, blank and shifting, just beyond the first post.

Then Dixie lifted his head and gazed questioningly before him, his ears pointed forward—sentient, strained—and whinnied shrill challenge. He hurried his steps, dragging Chub out of the beginnings of a dream. Vaughan straightened and took his hands from his pockets.

Out beyond the dim, wavering outline of the farthest post came answer to the challenge. A mysterious, vague shape grew impalpably upon the strained vision; a horse sneezed, then nickered eagerly. Vaughan drew up and waited.

"Hello!" he called cheerfully. "Pleasant day, this. Out for your health?"

The shape hesitated, as though taken aback by the greeting, and there was no answer. Vaughan, puzzled, rode closer.

"Say, don't talk so fast!" he yelled. "I can't follow yuh."

"Who—who is it?" The voice sounded perturbed; and it was, moreover, the voice of a woman.

Vaughan pulled up short and swore into his collar. Women are not, as a rule, to be met out on the blank prairie in a blizzard. His voice, when he spoke again, was not ironical, as it had been; it was placating.

"I beg your pardon," he said. "I thought it was a man. I'm looking for the Cross L; you don't happen to know where it is, do yuh?"

"No—I don't," she declared dismally. "I don't know where any place is. I'm teaching school in this neighborhood—or in some other. I was going to spend Sunday with a friend, but this storm came up, and I'm—lost."

"Same here," said Rowdy pleasantly, as though being lost was a matter for congratulation.

"Oh! I was in hopes—"

"So was I, so we're even there. We'll have to pool our chances, I guess. Any gate down that way—or haven't you followed the fence?"

"I followed it for miles and miles—it seemed. It must be some big field of the Cross L; but they have so very many big fields!"

"And you couldn't give a rough guess at how far it is to the Cross L?"—insinuatingly.

He could vaguely see her shake of head. "Ordinarily it should be about six miles beyond Rodway's, where I board. But I haven't the haziest idea of where Rodway's place is, you see; so that won't help you much. I'm all at sea in this snow." Her voice was rueful.

"Well, if you came up the fence, there's no use going back that way; and there's sure nothing made by going away from it.—that's the way I came. Why not go on the way you're headed?"

"We might as well, I suppose," she assented; and Rowdy turned and rode by her side, grateful for the plurality of the pronoun which tacitly included him in her wanderings, and meditating many things. For one, he wondered if she were as nice a girl as her voice sounded. He could not see much of her face, because it was muffled in a white silk scarf. Only her eyes showed, and they were dark and bright.

When he awoke to the fact that the wind, grown colder, beat upon her cruelly, he dropped behind a pace and took the windy side, that he might shield her with his body. But if she observed the action she gave no sign; her face was turned from him and the wind, and she rode without speaking. After long plodding, the line of posts turned unexpectedly a right angle, and Vaughan took a long, relieved breath.

"We'll have the wind on our backs now," he remarked. "I guess we may as well keep on and see where this fence goes to."

His tone was too elaborately cheerful to be very cheering. He was wondering if the girl was dressed warmly. It had been so warm and sunny before the blizzard struck, but now the wind searched out the thin places in one's clothing and ran lead in one's bones, where should be simply marrow. He fancied that her voice, when she spoke, gave evidence of actual suffering—and the heart of Rowdy Vaughan was ever soft toward a woman.

"If you're cold," he began, "I'll open up my bed and get out a blanket." He held Dixie in tentatively.

"Oh, don't trouble to do that," she protested; but there was that in her voice which hardened his impulse into fixed resolution.

"I ought to have thought of it before," he lamented, and swung down stiffly into the snow.

Her eyes followed his movement with a very evident interest while he unbuckled the pack Chub had carried since sunrise and drew out a blanket.

"Stand in your stirrup," he commanded briskly "and I'll wrap you up. It's a Navajo, and the wind will have a time trying to find a thin spot."

"You're thoughtful." She snuggled into it thankfully. "I was cold."

Vaughan tucked it around her with more care than haste. He was pretty uncomfortable himself, and for that reason he was the more anxious that the girl should be warm. It came to him that she was a cute little schoolma'am, all right; he was glad she belonged close around the Cross L. He also wished he knew her name—and so he set about finding it out, with much guile.

"How's that?" he wanted to know, when he had made sure that her feet—such tiny feet—were well covered. He thought it lucky that she did not ride astride, after the manner of the latter-day young woman, because then he could not have covered her so completely. "Hold on! That windy side's going to make trouble." He unbuckled the strap he wore to hold his own coat snug about him, and put it around the girl's slim waist, feeling idiotically happy and guilty the while. "It don't come within a mile of you," he complained; "but it'll help some."

Sheltered in the thick folds of the Navajo, she laughed, and the sound of it sent the blood galloping through Rowdy Vaughan's body so that he was almost warm. He went and scraped the snow out of his saddle, and swung up, feeling that, after all, there are worse things in the world than being lost and hungry in a blizzard, with a sweet-voiced, bright-eyed little schoolma'am who can laugh like that.

"I don't want to have you think I may be a bold, bad robber-man," he said, when they got going again. "My name's Rowdy Vaughan—for which I beg your pardon. Mother named me Rowland, never knowing I'd get out here and have her nice, pretty name mutilated that way. I won't say that my behavior never suggested the change, though. I'm from the Horseshoe Bar, over the line, and if I have my way, I'll be a Cross L man before another day." Then he waited expectantly.

"For fear you may think I'm a—a robber-woman," she answered him solemnly—he felt sure her eyes twinkled, if only he could have seen them— "I'm Jessie Conroy. And if you're from over the line, maybe you know my brother Harry. He was over there a year or two."

Rowdy hunched his shoulders—presumably at the wind. Harry Conroy's sister, was she? And he swore. "I may have met him," he parried, in a tone you'd never notice as being painstakingly careless. "I think I did, come to think of it."

Miss Conroy seemed displeased, and presently the cause was forthcoming. "If you'd ever met him," she said, "you'd hardly forget him." (Rowdy mentally agreed profanely.) "He's the best rider in the whole country—and the handsomest. He—he's splendid! And he's the only brother I've got. It's a pity you never got acquainted with him."

"Yes," lied Rowdy, and thought a good deal in a very short time. Harry Conroy's sister! Well, she wasn't to blame for that, of course; nor for thinking her brother a white man. "I remember I did see him ride once," he observed. "He was a whirlwind, all right—and he sure was handsome, too."

Miss Conroy turned her face toward him and smiled her pleasure, and Rowdy hovered between heaven and—another place. He was glad she smiled, and he was afraid of what that subject might discover for his straightforward tongue in the way of pitfalls. It would not be nice to let her know what he really thought of her brother.

"This looks to me like a lane," he said diplomatically. "We must be getting somewhere; don't you recognize any landmarks?"

Miss Conroy leaned forward and peered through the clouds of snow dust. Already the night was creeping down upon the land, stealthily turning the blank white of the blizzard into as blank a gray—which was as near darkness as it could get, because of the snow which fell and fell, and yet seemed never to find an abiding-place, but danced and swirled giddily in the wind as the cold froze it dry. There would be no more damp, clinging masses that night; it was sifting down like flour from a giant sieve; and of the supply there seemed no end.

"I don't know of any lanes around here," she began dubiously, "unless it's—"

Vaughan looked sharply at her muffled figure and wondered why she broke off so suddenly. She was staring hard at the few, faint traces of landmarks; and, bundled in the red-and-yellow Navajo blanket, with her bright, dark eyes, she might easily have passed for a slim young squaw.

Out ahead, a dog began barking vaguely, and Rowdy turned eagerly to the sound. Dixie, scenting human habitation, stepped out more briskly through the snow, and even Chub lifted an ear briefly to show he heard.

"It may not be any one you know," Vaughan remarked, and his voice showed his longing; "but it'll be shelter and a warm fire—and supper. Can you appreciate such blessings, Miss Conroy? I can. I've been in the saddle since sunrise; and I was so sure I'd strike the Cross L by dinner-time that I didn't bring a bite to eat. It was a sheep-camp where I stopped, and the grub didn't look good to me, anyway—I've called myself bad names all the afternoon for being more dainty than sensible. But it's all right now, I guess."

CHAPTER 2.
Miss Conroy Refuses Shelter.

The storm lifted suddenly, as storms have a way of doing, and a low, squat ranch-house stood dimly revealed against the bleak expanse of wind-tortured prairie. Rowdy gave an exultant little whoop and made for the gate, leaned and swung it open and rode through, dragging Chub after him by main strength, as usual. When he turned to close the gate after Miss Conroy he found her standing still in the lane.

"Come on in," he called, with a trace of impatience born of his weariness and hunger.

"Thank you, no." Miss Conroy's voice was as crisply cold as the wind which fluttered the Navajo blanket around her face. "I much prefer the blizzard."

For a moment Rowdy found nothing to say; he just stared. Miss Conroy shifted uneasily in the saddle.

"This is old Bill Brown's place," she explained reluctantly. "He—I'd rather freeze than go in!"

"Well, I guess that won't be hard to do," he retorted curtly, "if you stay out much longer."

The dog was growing hysterical over their presence, and Bill Brown himself came out to see what it was all about. He could see two dim figures at the gate.

"Hello!" he shouted. "Why don't yuh come on in? What yuh standing there chewing the rag for?"

Vaughan hesitated, his eyes upon Miss Conroy.

"Go in," she commanded imperiously, quite as if he were a refractory pupil. "You're tired out, and hungry. I'm neither. Besides, I know where I am now. I can find my way without any trouble. Go in, I tell you!"

But Rowdy stayed where he was, with the gate creaking to and fro between them. Dixie circled till his back was to the wind. "I hope you don't think you're going to mill around out here alone," Rowdy said tartly.

"I can manage very well. I'm not lost now, I tell you. Rodway's is only three miles from here, and I know the direction."

Bill Brown waded out to them, wondering what weighty discussion was keeping them there in the cold. Vaughan he passed by with the cursory glance of a disinterested stranger, and went on to where Miss Conroy waited stubbornly in the lane.

"Oh, it's you!" he said grimly. "Well, come in and thaw out; I hope yuh didn't think yuh wouldn't be welcome yuh knew better. You got lost, I reckon. Come on—"

Miss Conroy struck Badger sharply across the flank and disappeared into the night. "When I ask shelter of you," she flung back, "you'll know it."

Rowdy started after, and met Bill Brown squarely in the gate. Bill eyed him sharply. "Say, young fellow, how'd you come by that packhorse?" he demanded, as Chub brushed past him.

"None of your damn' business," snapped Rowdy, and drove the spurs into Dixie's ribs. But Chub was a handicap at any time; now, when he was tired, there was no getting anything like speed out of him; he clung to his shuffling trot, which was really no better than a walk. After five minutes spent alternately in spurring Dixie and yanking at Chub's lead-rope, Rowdy grew frightened and took to shouting. While they were in the lane Miss Conroy must perforce ride straight ahead, but the lane would not last always. As though with malicious intent, the snow swooped down again and the world became an unreal, nightmare world, wherein was nothing save shifting, blinding snowfloury and wind and bitter, numbing cold.

Rowdy stood in his stirrups, cupped his chilled fingers around his numbed lips, and sent a longdrawn "Who-ee!" shrilling weirdly into the night.

It seemed to him, after long listening, that from the right came faint reply, and he turned and rode recklessly, swearing at Chub for his slowness. He called again, and the answer, though faint, was unmistakable. He settled heavily into the saddle—too weak, from sheer relief, to call again. He had not known till then just how frightened he had been, and he was somewhat disconcerted at the discovery. In a minute the reaction passed and he shouted a loud hello.

"Hello?" came the voice of Miss Conroy, tantalizingly calm, and as superior as the greeting of Central. "Were you looking for me, Mr. Vaughan?"

She was close to him—so close that she had not needed to raise her voice perceptibly. Rowdy rode up alongside, remembering uncomfortably his prolonged shouting.

"I sure was," he admitted. And then: "You rode off with my blanket on." He was very proud of his matter-of-fact tone.

"Oh!" Miss Conroy was almost deceived, and a bit disappointed. "I'll give it to you now, and you can go back—if you know the way."

"No hurry," said Rowdy politely. "I'll go on and see if you can find a place that looks good to you. You seem pretty particular."

Miss Conroy may have blushed, in the shelter of the blanket. "I suppose it did look strange to you," she confessed, but defiantly. "Bill Brown is an enemy to—Harry. He—because he lost a horse or two out of a field, one time, he—he actually accused Harry of taking them! He lied, of course, and nobody believed him; nobody could believe a thing like that about Harry. It was perfectly absurd. But he did his best to hurt Harry's name, and I would rather freeze than ask shelter of him. Wouldn't you—in my place, I mean?"

"I always stand up for my friends," evaded Rowdy. "And if I had a brother—"

"Of course you'd be loyal," approved Miss Conroy warmly. "But I didn't want you to come on; it isn't your quarrel. And I know the way now. You needn't have come any farther."

"You forgot the blanket," Rowdy reminded wickedly. "I think a lot of that Navajo."

"You insisted upon my taking it," she retorted, and took refuge in silence.

For a long hour they plodded blindly. Rowdy beat his hands often about his body to start the blood, and meditated yearnigly upon hot coffee and the things he liked best to eat. Also, a good long pull at a flask wouldn't be had, either, he thought. And he hoped this little schoolma'am knew where she was going—truth to tell, he doubted it.

After a while, it seemed that Miss Conroy doubted it also. She took to leaning forward and straining her eyes to see through the gray wall before.

"There should be a gate here," she said dubiously, at last.

"It seems to me," Rowdy ventured mildly, "if there were a gate, it would have some kind of a fence hitched to it; wouldn't it?"

Miss Conroy was in no mood for facetiousness, and refused to answer his question. "I surely can't have made a mistake," she observed uneasily.

"It would be a wonder if you didn't, such a night as this," he consoled. "I wouldn't bank on traveling straight myself, even if I knew the country—which I don't. And I've been in more blizzards than I'm years old."

"Rodway's place can't be far away," she said, brightening. "It may be farther to the east; shall we try that way—if you know which is east?"

"Sure, we'll try. It's all we can do. My packhorse is about all in, from the way he hangs back; if we don't strike something pretty soon I'll have to turn him loose."

"Oh, don't do that," she begged. "It would be too cruel. We're sure to reach Rodway's very soon."

More plodding through drifts high and drifts low; more leaning from saddles to search anxiously for trace of something besides snow and wind and biting cold. Then, far to the right, a yellow eye glowed briefly when the storm paused to take breath. Miss Conroy gave a glad little cry and turned Badger sharply.

"Did you see? It was the light from a window. We were going the wrong way. I'm sure that is Rodway's."

Rowdy thanked the Lord and followed her. They came up against a fence, found a gate, and passed through. While they hurried toward it, the light winked welcome; as they drew near, some one stirred the fire and sent sparks and rose-hued smoke rushing up into the smother of snow. Rowdy watched them wistfully, and wondered if there would be supper, and strong, hot coffee. He lifted Miss Conroy out of the saddle, carried her two long strides, and deposited her upon the door-step; rapped imperatively, and when a voice replied, lifted the latch and pushed her in before him.

For a minute they stood blinking, just within the door. The change from numbing cold and darkness to the light of the overheated room was stupefying.

Then Miss Conroy went over and held her little, gloved hands to the heat of the stove, but she did not take the chair which some one pushed toward her. She stood, the blanket shrouding her face and her slim young figure, and looked about her curiously. It was not Rodway's house, after all. She thought she knew what place it was—the shack where Rodway's hay-balers bached.

From the first, Rowdy did not like the look of things—though for himself it did not matter; he was used to such scenes. It was the presence of the girl which made him uncomfortable. He unbuttoned his coat that the warmth might reach his chilled body, and frowned.

Four men sat around a small, dirty table; evidently the arrivals had interrupted an exciting game of seven-up. A glance told Rowdy, even if his nose had not, that the four round, ribbed bottles had not been nearly emptied without effect.

"Have one on the house," the man nearest him cried, and shoved a bottle toward him.

Involuntarily Rowdy reached for it. Now that he was inside, he realized all at once how weary he was, and cold and hungry. Each abused muscle and nerve seemed to have a distinct grievance against him. His fingers closed around the bottle before he remembered and dropped it. He looked up, hoping Miss Conroy had not observed the action; met her wide, questioning eyes, and the blood flew guiltily to his cheeks.

"Thanks, boys—not any for me," he said, and apologized to Miss Conroy with his eyes.

The man rose and confronted him unsteadily. "Dat's a hell off a way! You too proud for drink weeth us? You drink, now! By Gar, I make you drink!"

Rowdy's eyelids drooped, which was a bad sign for those who knew him. "You're forgetting there's a lady present," he reminded warningly.

The man turned a brief, contemptuous glance toward the stove. "You got the damn' queer way to talk. I don't call no squaw no lady. You drink queeck, now!"

"Aw, shut up, Frenchy," the man at his elbow abjured him. "He don't have to drink if he don't want to."

"You keep the face close," the other retorted majestically; and cursed loud and long and incoherently.

Rowdy drew back his arm, with a fist that meant trouble for somebody; but there were others before him who pinned the importunate host to the table, where he squirmed unavailingly.

Rowdy buttoned up his coat the while he eyed the group disgustedly. "I guess we'll drift," he remarked. "You don't look good to me, and that's no dream."

"Aw, stay and warm up," the fourth man expostulated. "Yuh don't need t' mind Le Febre; he's drunk."

But Rowdy opened the door decisively, and Miss Conroy, her cheeks like two storm-buffeted poppies, followed him out with dignity—albeit trailing a yard of red-and-yellow Navajo blanket behind her. Rowdy lifted her into the saddle, tucked her feet carefully under the blanket, and said never a word.

"Mr. Vaughan," she began hesitatingly, "this is too bad; you need not have left. I—I wasn't afraid."

"I know you weren't," conceded Rowdy. "But it was a hard formation—for a woman. Are there any more places on this flat marked Unavailable?"

Miss Conroy replied misanthropically that if there were they would be sure to find them.

They took up their weary wanderings again, while the yellow eye of the window winked after them. They missed Rodway's by a scant hundred yards, and didn't know it, because the side of the house next them had no lighted windows. They traveled in a wide, half circle, and thought that they were leaving a straight trail behind them. More than once Rowdy was urged by his aching arm to drop the lead-rope and leave Chub to shift by himself, but habit was strong and his heart was soft. Then he felt an odd twitching at the lead-rope, as if Chub were minded to rebel against their leadership. Rowdy yanked him into remembrance of his duty, and wondered. Bill Brown's question came insistently to mind; he wondered the more.

Two minutes and the lead-rope was sawing against the small of his back again. Rowdy turned Dixie's head, and spoke for the first time in an hour.

"My packhorse seems to have an idea about where he wants to go," he said. "I guess we might as well follow him as anybody; he ain't often taken with a rush of brains to the head. And we can't be any worse lost than we are now, can we?"

Miss Conroy said no dispiritedly, and they swung about and followed Chub's leadership apathetically. It took Chub just five minutes to demonstrate that he knew what he was about. When he stopped, it was with his nose against a corral gate; not content with that, he whinnied, and a new, exultant note was in the sound. A deep-voiced dog bayed loudly, and a shrill yelp cut in and clamored for recognition.

Miss Conroy gasped. "It's Lion and Skeesicks. We're at Rodway's, Mr. Vaughan."

Rowdy, for the second time, thanked the Lord. But when he was stripping the pack off Chub's back, ten minutes later, he was thinking many things he would not have cared to say aloud. It might be all right, but it sure was strange, he told himself, that Chub belonged here at Rodway's when Harry Conroy claimed that he was an Oregon horse. Rowdy had thought his account against Harry Conroy long enough, but it looked now as though another item must be added to the list. He went in and ate his supper thoughtfully, and when he got into bed he did not fall asleep within two minutes, as he might be expected to do. His last conscious thought was not of stolen horses, however. It was: "And she's Harry Conroy's sister! Now, what do you think of that? But all the same, she's sure a nice little schoolma'am."

CHAPTER 3.
Rowdy Hires a New Boss.

Next morning, after breakfast, Mr. Rodway followed Vaughan out to the stable, and repeated Bill Brown's question.

"I'd like to know where yuh got this horse," he began, with an apologetic sort of determination in his tone. "He happens to belong to me. He was run off with a bunch three years ago, and this is the first trace anybody has ever got of 'em. I see the brand's been worked. It was a Roman four—that's my brand; now it looks like a map of Texas; but I'd swear to the horse—raised him from a colt."

Rowdy had expected something of the sort, and he knew quite well what he was going to do; he had settled that the night before, with the memory of Miss Conroy's eyes fresh in his mind.

"I got him in a deal across the line," he said. "I was told he came from east Oregon. But last night, when he piloted us straight to your corral gate, I guessed he'd been here before. He's yours, all right, if you say so."

"Uh course he ain't worth such a pile uh money," apologized Rodway, "but the kids thought a heap of him. I'd rather locate some of the horses that was with him—or the man yuh got him of. They was some mighty good horses run out uh this country then, but they was all out on the range, so we didn't miss 'em in time to do any good. Do yu know who took 'em across the line?"

"No," said Rowdy deliberately. "The man I got Chub from went north, and I heard he got killed. I don't know of any other in the deal."

Rodway grunted, and Vaughan began vigorously brushing Dixie's roughened coat. "If you don't mind," he said, after a minute, "I'd like to borrow Chub to pack my bed over to the Cross L. I can bring him back again."

"Why, sure!" assented Rodway eagerly. "I hate to take him from yuh, but the kids—"

"Oh, that's all right," interrupted Rowdy cheerfully. "It's all in the game, and I should 'a' looked up his pedigree, for I knew—. Anyway, was worth the price of him to have him along last night. We'd have milled around till daylight, I guess, only for him."

"That's what," agreed Rodway. "Jessie's horse is one she brought from home lately, and he ain't located yet; I dunno as he'd 'a' piloted her home. Billy— that's what the kids named him—was born and raised here, yuh see. I'll bet he's glad to get back—and the kids'll be plumb wild."

Rowdy did not answer; there seemed nothing in particular to say, and he was wondering if he would see Miss Conroy before he left. She had not eaten breakfast with the others; from their manner, he judged that no one expected her to. He was not well informed upon the subject of schoolma'ams, but he had a hazy impression that late rising was a distinguishing characteristic— and he did not know how late. He saddled leisurely, and packed his bed for the last time upon Chub. The red-and-yellow Navajo blanket he folded tenderly, with an unconscious smile for the service it had done, and laid it in its accustomed place in the bed. Then, having no plausible excuse for going back to the house, he mounted and rode away into the brilliant white world, watching wistfully the house from the tail of his eye.

She might have got up in time to see him off, he thought discontentedly; but he supposed one cowpuncher more or less made little difference to her. Anyway, he didn't know as he had any license to moon around her. She probably had a fellow; she might even be engaged, for all he knew. And— she was Harry Conroy's sister; and from his experience with the breed, good looks didn't count for anything. Harry was good-looking, and he was a snake, if ever there was one. He had never expected to lie for him—but he had done it, all right—and because Harry's sister happened to have nice eyes and a pretty little foot!—

He had half a mind to go back and tell Rodway all he knew about those horses; it was only a matter of time, anyway, till Harry Conroy overshot the mark and got what was coming to him. He sure didn't owe Harry anything, that he had need to shield him like he had done. Still, Rodway would wonder why he hadn't told it at first; and that little girl believed in Harry, and said he was "splendid!" Humph! He wondered if he really meant that. If she did—

He squared his back to the house—and the memory of Miss Conroy's eyes— and plodded across the field to the gate. Now the sun was shining, and there was no possibility of getting lost. The way to the Cross L lay straight and plain before him.

Rowdy rode leisurely up over the crest of a ridge beyond which lay the home ranch of the Cross L. Whether it was henceforth to be his home he had yet to discover—though there was reason for hoping that it would be. Even so venturesome a man as Rowdy Vaughan would scarce ride a long hundred miles through unpeopled prairie, in the tricky month of March, without some reason for expecting a welcome at the end of his journey. In this case, a previous acquaintance with "Wooden Shoes" Mielke, foreman of the Cross L, was Rowdy's trump-card. Wooden Shoes, whenever chance had brought them together in the last two or three years, was ever urging Rowdy to come over and unroll his soogans in the Cross L bed-tent, and promising the best string in the outfit to ride—besides other things alluring to a cow-puncher.

So that, when his relations with the Horseshoe Bar became strained, Rowdy remembered his friend of the Cross L and the promises, and had drifted south.

Just now he hoped that Wooden Shoes would be home to greet him, and his eyes searched wishfully the huddle of low-eaved cabins and the assortment of sheds and corrals for the bulky form of the foreman. But no one seemed to be about—except a bigbodied, bandy-legged individual, who appeared to be playfully chasing a big, bright bay stallion inside the large enclosure where stood the cabins.

Rowdy watched them impersonally; a glance proved that the man was not Wooden Shoes, and so he was not particularly interested in him or his doings. It did occur to him, however, that if the fellow wanted to catch that brute, he ought to have sense enough to get a horse. No one but a plumb idiot would mill around in that snow afoot. He jogged down the slope at a shuffling trot, grinning tolerantly at the pantomime below.

He of the bandy-legs stopped, evidently out of breath; the stallion stopped also, snorting defiance. Rowdy heard him plainly, even at that distance. The horse arched his neck and watched the man warily, ready to be off at the first symptom of hostilities—and Rowdy observed that a short rope hung from his halter, swaying as he moved.

Bandy-legs seemed to have an idea; he turned and scuttled to the nearest cabin, returning with what seemed a basin of oats, for he shook it enticingly and edged cautiously toward the horse. Rowdy could imagine him coaxing, with hypocritically endearing names, such as "Good old boy!" and "Steady now, Billy"—or whatever the horse's name might be. Rowdy chuckled to himself, and hoped the horse saw through the subterfuge.

Perhaps the horse chuckled also; at any rate, he stood quite still, equally prepared to bounce away on the instant or to don the mask of docility. Bandy-legs drew nearer and nearer, shaking the basin briskly, like an old woman sifting meal. The horse waited, his nostrils quivering hungrily at the smell of the oats, and with an occasional low nicker.

Bandy-legs went on tiptoes—or as nearly as he could in the snow—the basin at arm's length before. The dainty, flaring nostrils sniffed tentatively, dipped into the basin, and snuffed the oats about luxuriously—till he felt a stealthy hand seize the dangling rope. At the touch he snorted protest, and was off and away, upsetting Bandy-legs and the basin ignominiously into a high-piled drift.

Bandy-legs sat up, scraped the snow out of his collar and his ears, and swore. It was then that Rowdy appeared like an angel of deliverance.

"Want that horse caught?" he yelled cheerfully.

Bandy-legs lifted up his voice and bellowed things I should not like to repeat verbatim. But Rowdy gathered that the man emphatically did want that so-and-so-and-then-some horse caught, and that it couldn't be done a blessed minute too soon. Whereat Rowdy smiled anew, with his face discreetly turned away from Bandy-legs, and took down his rope and widened the loop. Also, he turned Chub loose.

The stallion evidently sensed what new danger threatened his stolen freedom, and circled the yard with high, springy strides. Rowdy circled after, saw his chance, swirled the loop twice over his head, and hazarded a long throw.

Rowdy knew it for pure good luck that it landed right, but to this day Bandy-legs looks upon him as a Wonder with a rope—and Bandy-legs would insist upon the capital.

"Where shall I take him?" Rowdy asked, coming up with his captive, and with nothing but his eyes to show how he was laughing inwardly.

Bandy-legs crawled from the drift, still scraping snow from inside his collar, and gave many directions about going through a certain gate into such-and-such a corral; from there into a stable; and by seeming devious ways into a minutely described stall.

"All right," said Rowdy, cutting short the last needless details. "I guess I can find the trail;" and started off, leading the stallion. Bandy-legs followed, and Chub, observing the departure of Dixie, ambled faithfully in the rear.

"Much obliged," conceded Bandy-legs, when the stallion was safely housed and tied securely. "Where yuh headed for, young man?"

"Right here," Rowdy told him calmly, loosening Dixie's cinch. "I'm the long-lost top hand that the Cross L's been watching the sky-line for, lo! these many moons, a-yearning for the privilege of handing me forty plunks about twice as fast as I've got 'em coming. Where's the boss?"

"Er—I'm him," confessed Bandy-legs meekly, and circled the two dubiously. "I guess you've heard uh Eagle Creek Smith—I'm him. The Cross L belongs to me."

Rowdy let out an explosive, and showed a row of nice teeth. "Well, I ain't hard to please," he added. "I won't kick on that, I guess. I like your looks tolerable well, and I'm willing to take yuh on for a boss. If yuh do your part, I bet we'll get along fine." His tone was banteringly patronizing "Anyway, I'll try yuh for a spell. You can put my name down as Rowdy Vaughan, lately canned from the Horseshoe Bar."

"What for?" ventured Bandy-legs—rather, Eagle Creek—still circling Rowdy dubiously.

"What for was I canned?" repeated Rowdy easily. "Being a modest youth, I hate t' tell yuh. But the old man's son and me, we disagreed, and one of his eyes swelled some; so did mine, a little." He stood head and shoulders above Eagle Creek, and he smiled down upon him engagingly. Eagle Creek capitulated before the smile.

"Well, I ain't got any sons—that I know of," he grinned. "So I guess yuh can consider yourself a Cross L man till further notice."

"Why, sure!" The teeth gleamed again briefly. "That's what I've been telling you right along. Where's old Wooden Shoes? He's responsible for me being here."

"Gone to Chinook. He'll be back in a day or two." Eagle Creek shifted his feet awkwardly. "Say"—he glanced uneasily behind him—"yuh don't want t' let it get around that yuh sort of—hired me—see?"

"Of course not," Rowdy assured him. "I was only joshing. If you don't want me, just tell me to hit the sod."

"You stay right where you're at!" commanded Eagle Creek with returned confidence in himself and his authority. Of a truth, this self-assured, straight-limbed young man had rather dazed him. "Take your bed and war-bag up to the bunk-house and make yourself t' home till the boys get back, and—say, where'd yuh git that pack-horse?"

The laugh went out of Rowdy's tawny eyes. The question hit a spot that was becoming sore. "I borrowed him this morning from Mr. Rodway," he said evenly. "I'm to take him back to-day. I stopped there last night."

"Oh!" Eagle Creek coughed apologetically, and said no word, while Rowdy led Chub back to the cabin which he had pointed out as the bunk-house; he stood by while Rowdy loosened the pack and dragged it inside.

"I guess you can get located here," he said. "I ain't workin' more'n three or four men just now, but there's quite a few uh the boys stopping here; the Cross L's a regular hang-out for cow-punchers. You're a little early for the season, but I'll see that yuh have something t' do—just t' keep yuh out uh devilment."

Rowdy's brows unbent; it would seem that Eagle Creek was capable of "joshing" also. "It's up t' you, old-timer," he retorted. "I'm strong and willing, and don't shy at anything but pitchforks."

Eagle Creek grinned. "This ain't no blamed cowhospital," he gave as a parting shot. "All the hay that's shoveled on this ranch needn't hurt nobody's feelings." With that he shut the door, and left Rowdy to acquaint himself with his new home.

CHAPTER 4.
Pink as "Chappyrone."

Rowdy was sprawled ungracefully upon somebody's bunk—he neither knew nor cared whose—and he was snoring unmelodiously, and not dreaming a thing; for when a cow-puncher has nothing in particular to do, he sleeps to atone for the weary hours when he must be very wide-awake. An avalanche descended upon his unwarned middle, and checked the rhythmic ebb and flow of sound. He squawked and came to life clawing viciously.

"I'd like t' know where the devil yuh come from," a voice remarked plaintively in a soft treble.

Rowdy opened his eyes with a snap. "Pink! by all that's good and bad! Get up off my diaphragm, you little fiend."

Pink absent-mindedly kneaded Rowdy's stomach with his knuckles, and immediately found himself in a far corner. He came back, dimpling mischievously. He looked much more an angel than a fiend, for all his Angora chaps and flame-colored scarf.

"Your bed and war-bag's on my bunk; you're on Smoky's; and Dixie's makin' himself to home in the corral. By all them signs and tokens, I give a reckless guess you're here t' stay a while. That right?" He prodded again at Rowdy's ribs.

"It sure is, Pink. And if I'd known you was holding out here, I'd 'a' come sooner, maybe. You sure look good to me, you darned little cuss!" Rowdy sat up and took a lightning inventory of the four or five other fellows lounging about. He must have slept pretty sound, he thought, not to hear them come in.

Pink read the look, and bethought him of the necessary introductions. "This is my side-kicker over the line that—you've heard about till you're plumb weary, boys," he announced musically. "His name is Rowdy Vaughan—bronco-peeler, crap fiend, and all-round bad man. He ain't a safe companion, and yuh want t' sleep with your six-guns cuddled under your right ear, and never, on no account, show him your backs. He's a real wolf, he is, and the only reason I live t' tell the tale is because he respects m' size. Boys, I'm afraid for yuh—but I wish yuh well."

"Pink, you need killing, and I'm tempted to live up to my rep," grinned Rowdy indulgently. "Read me the pedigree of your friends."

"Oh, they ain't no worse—when yuh git used to 'em. That long-legged jasper with the far-away look in his eyes is the Silent One—if he takes a notion t' you, he'll maybe tell yuh the name his mother calls him. He may have seen better days; but here's hoping he won't see no worse! He once was a tenderfoot; but he's convalescing."

The Silent One nodded carelessly, but with a quick, measuring glance that Rowdy liked.

"This unshaved savage is Smoky. He's harmless, if yuh don't mention socialism in his presence; and if yuh do, he'll down-with-the-trust-and-long-live-the-sons-uh-toil, all hours uh the night, and keep folks awake. Then him and the fellow that started him off 'll likely get chapped good and plenty. Over there's Jim Ellis and Bob Nevin; they've both turned a cow or two, and I've seen worse specimens running around loose—plenty of 'em. That man hidin' behind the grin—you can see him if yuh look close—is Sunny Sam. Yuh needn't take no notice of him, unless you're a mind to. He won't care—he's dead gentle.

"Say," he broke off, "how'd you happen t' stray onto this range, anyhow? Yuh used t' belong t the Horseshoe Bar so solid the assessor always t' yuh down on the personal-property list."

"They won't pay taxes on me no more, son." Rowdy's eyes dwelt fondly upon Pink's cupid-bow mouth and dimples. He had never dreamed of finding Pink here; though, when he came to think of it there was no reason why he shouldn't.

Pink was not like any one else. He was slight and girlish to look at. But you mustn't trust appearances; for Pink was all muscle strung on steel wire, according to the belief of those who tried to handle him. He had little white hands, and feet that looked quite comfortable in a number four boot, and his hair was a tawny gold and curled in distracting, damp rings on his forehead. His eyes were blue and long-lashed and beautiful, and they looked at the world with baby innocence—whereas a more sophisticated little devil never jangled spurs at his heels. He was everything but insipid, and men liked him—unless he chose to dislike them, when they thought of him with grating teeth. To find him bullying the Cross L boys brought a warmth to Rowdy's heart.

Pink made a cigarette, and then offered Rowdy his tobacco-sack, and asked questions about the Cypress Hills country. How was this girl?—and was that one married yet?—and did the other still grieve for him? As a matter of fact, he had yet to see the girl who could quicken his pulse a single beat, and for that reason it sometimes pleased him to affect susceptibility beyond that of other men.

It was after dinner when he and Rowdy went humming down to the stables, gossiping like a couple of old women over a back fence.

"I see you've got Conroy's Chub yet," Pink observed carelessly.

"Oh, for Heaven's sake let up on that cayuse!" Rowdy cried petulantly. "I wish I'd never got sight of the little buzzard-head; I've had him crammed down my throat the last day or two till it's getting plumb monotonous. Pink, that cayuse never saw Oregon. He was raised right on this flat, and he belongs to old Rodway. I've got to lead him back there and turn him over to-day."

Pink took three puffs at his cigarette, and lifted his long lashes to Rowdy's gloom-filled face. "Stole?" he asked briefly.

"Stole," Rowdy repeated disgustedly. "So was the whole blame' bunch, as near as I can make out."

"We might 'a' knowed it. We might 'a' guessed Harry Conroy wouldn't have a straight title to anything if he could make it crooked. I bet he never finished paying back that money yuh lent him—out uh the kindness uh your heart. Did he?" Pink leaned against the corral fence and kicked meditatively at a snow-covered rock.

"He did not, m' son. Chub's all I ever got out uh the deal—and I haven't even got him. I borrowed him from Rodway to pack my bed over—borrowed the blame' little runty cayuse that cost me sixty-four hard-earned dollars; that's what Harry borrowed of me. And every blame' gazabo on the flat wanted to know what I was doing with him!"

"I can tell yuh where t' find Conroy, Rowdy. He's working for an outfit down on the river. I'd sure fix him for this! Yuh got plenty of evidence; you can send him up like a charm. It was different when he cut your latigo strap in that rough-riding contest; yuh couldn't prove it on him. But this—why, man, it's a cinch!"

"I haven't lost Harry Conroy, so I ain't looking for him just now," growled Rowdy. "So long as he keeps out uh reach, I won't ask no more of him. And, Pink, I wish you'd keep this quiet—about him having Chub. I told Rodway I couldn't put him next to the fellow that brought that bunch across the line. I told him the fellow went north and got killed. He did go north—fifty miles or so; and he'd ought to been killed, if he wasn't. Let it go that way, Pink."

Pink looked like a cherub-faced child when he has been told there's no Santa Claus. "Sure, if yuh say so," he stammered dubiously. He eyed Rowdy reproachfully, and then looked away to the horizon. He kicked the rock out of place, and then poked it painstakingly back with his toe—and from the look of him, he did not know there was a rock there at all.

"How'd yuh happen to run across Rodway?" he asked guilelessly.

"I stopped there last night. I got to milling around in that storm, and ran across the schoolma'am that boards at Rodway's, She was plumb lost, too, so we dubbed around together for a while, and finally got inside Rodway's field. Then Chub come alive and piloted us to the house. This morning Rodway claimed him—says the brand has been worked from a Roman four. Oh, it's all straight goods," he added hastily. "Old Eagle Creek here knew him, too."

But Pink was not thinking of Chub. He hunched his chap-belt higher and spat viciously into the snow. "I knowed it," he declared, with melancholy triumph. "It's school-ma'amitis that's gave yuh softening uh the vitals, and not no Christian charity play. How comes it you're took that way, all unbeknown t' your friends? Yuh never used t' bother about no female girls. It's a cinch you're wise that she's Harry's sister; and I admit she's a swell looker. But so's he; and I should think, Rowdy, you'd had about enough uh that brand uh snake."

"There's nothing so snaky about her that I could see," defended Rowdy. He did not particularly relish having his own mental argument against Miss Conroy thrown back at him from another. "She seemed to be all right; and if you'd seen how plucky she was in that blizzard—"

"Well, I never heard anybody stand up and call Harry white-livered, when yuh come t' that," Pink cut in tartly. "Anyway, you're a blame fool. If she was a little white-winged angel, yuh wouldn't stand no kind uh show; and I tell yuh why. She's got a little tin god that she says prayers to regular."

"That's Harry. And wouldn't he be the fine brother-in-law? He could borrow all your wages off'n yuh, and when yuh went t' make a pretty ride, he'd up and cut your latigo, and give yuh a fall. And he could work stolen horses off onto yuh—and yuh wouldn't give a damn, 'cause Jessie wears a number two shoe—"

"You must have done some rimrock riding after her yourself!" jeered Rowdy.

"And has got shiny brown eyes, just like Harry's—"

"They're not!" laughed Rowdy, half-angrily. "If you say that again, Pink, I'll stick your head in a snow-bank. Her eyes are all right. They sure look good to me."

"You've sure got 'em," mourned Pink. "Yuh need t' be close-herded by your friends, and that's no dream. You wait till toward evening before yuh take that horse back. I'm going along t' chappyrone yuh, Rowdy. Yuh ain't safe running loose any more."

Rowdy cursed him companionably and told him to go along, if he wanted to, and to look out he didn't throw up his own hands; and Pink grumbled and swore and did go along. But when they got there, Miss Conroy greeted him like a very good friend; which sent Rowdy sulky, and kept him so all the evening. It seemed to him that Pink was playing a double game, and when they started home he told him so.

But Pink turned in his saddle and smiled so that his dimples showed plainly in the moonlight. "Chappyrones that set in a corner and look wise are the rankest kind uh fakes," he explained. "When she was talking to me, she was letting you alone—see?"

Rowdy accepted the explanation silently, and stored it away in his memory. After that, by riding craftily, and by threats, and by much vituperation, he managed to reach Rodway's unchapperoned at least three times out of five—which was doing remarkably well, when one considers Pink.

CHAPTER 5.
At Home at Cross L.

In two days Rowdy was quite at home with the Cross L. In a month he found himself transplanted from the smoke-laden air of the bunk-house, and set off from the world in a line camp, with nothing to do but patrol the boggy banks of Milk River, where it was still unfenced and unclaimed by small farmers. The only mitigation of his exile, so far as he could see, lay in the fact that he had Pink and the Silent One for companions.

It developed that when he would speak to the Silent One, he must say Jim, or wait long for a reply. Also, the Silent One was not always silent, and he was quick to observe the weak points in those around him, and keen at repartee. When it pleased him so to do, he could handle the English language in a way that was perfectly amazing—and not always intelligible to the unschooled. At such times Pink frankly made no attempt to understand him; Rowdy, having been hustled through grammar school and two-thirds through high school before he ran away from a brand new stepmother, rather enjoyed the outbreaks and Pink's consequent disgust.

Not one of them loved particularly the line camp, and Rowdy least of all, since it put an extra ten miles between Miss Conroy and himself. Rowdy had got to that point where his mind dwelt much upon matters domestic, and he made many secret calculations on the cost of housekeeping for two. More than that, he put himself upon a rigid allowance for pocket-money—an allowance barely sufficient to keep him in tobacco and papers. All this without consulting Miss Conroy's wishes—which only goes to show that Rowdy Vaughan was a born optimist.

The Silent One complained that he could not keep supplied with reading-matter, and Pink bewailed the monotony of inaction. For, beyond watching the river to keep the cattle from miring in the mud lately released from frost grip, there was nothing to do.

According to the calendar, spring was well upon them, and the prairies would soon be flaunting new dresses of green. The calendar, however, had neglected to record the rainless heat of the summer gone before, or the searing winds that burned the grass brown as it grew, or the winter which forgot its part and permitted prairie-dogs to chip-chip-chip above ground in January, when they should be sleeping decently in their cellar homes.

Apart from the brief storm which Rowdy had brought with him, there had been no snow worth considering. Always the chill winds shaved the barren land from the north, or veered unexpectedly, and blew dry warmth from the southwest; but never the snow for which the land yearned. Wind, and bright sunlight, and more wind, and hypocritical, drifting clouds, and more sun; lean cattle walking, walking, up-hill and down coulee, nose to the dry ground, snipping the stray tufts where should be a woolly carpet of sweet, ripened grasses, eating wildrose bushes level with the sod, and wishing there was only an abundance even of them; drifting uneasily from hilltop to farther hilltop, hunger-driven and gaunt, where should be sleek content. When they sought to continue their quest beyond the river, and the weaker bogged at its muddy edge, Rowdy and Pink and the Silent One would ride out, and with their ropes drag them back ignominiously to solid ground and the very doubtful joy of living.

May Day found the grass-land brown and lifeless, with a chill wind blowing over it. The cattle wandered as before except that knock-kneed little calves trailed beside their lean mothers and clamored for full stomachs.

The Cross L cattle bore the brunt of the range famine, because Eagle Creek Smith was a stockman of the old school. His cattle must live on the open range, because they always had done so. Other men bought or leased large tracts of grass-land, and fenced them for just such an emergency, but not he. It is true that he had two or three large fields, as Miss Conroy had told Rowdy, but it was his boast that all the hay he raised was eaten by his saddlehorses, and that all the fields he owned were used solely for horse pastures. The open range was the place for cattle and no Cross L critter ever fed inside a wire fence.

Through the dry summer before, when other men read the ominous signs and hurriedly leased pasture-land and cut down their herds to what the fields would feed, Eagle Creek went calmly on as he had done always. He shipped what beef was fit—and that, of a truth, was not much!—and settled down for the winter, trusting to winter snows and spring rains to refill the long-dry lakes and waterholes, and coat the levels anew with grass.

But the winter snows had failed to appear, and with the spring came no rain. "April showers" became a hideously ironical joke at nature's expense. Always the wind blew, and sometimes great flocks of clouds would drift superciliously up from the far sky-line, play with men's hopes, and sail disdainfully on to some more favored land.

It is all very well for a man to cling stubbornly to precedent, but if he clings long enough, there comes a time when to cling becomes akin to crime. Eagle Creek Smith still stubbornly held that rangecattle should be kept to the range. He waited until May was fast merging to June, watching, from sheer habit, for the spring transformation of brown prairies into green. When it did not come, and only the coulee sides and bottoms showed green among the brown, he accepted ruefully the unusual conditions which nature had thrust upon him, and started "Wooden Shoes" out with the wagons on the horse round-up, which is a preliminary to the roundup proper, as every one knows.

CHAPTER 6.
A Shot From the Dark.

"I call that a bad job well done," Pink remarked, after a long silence, as he gave over trying to catch a fish in the muddy Milk River.

"What?" Rowdy, still prone to day-dreams of matters domestic, came back reluctantly to reality, and inspected his bait.

"Oh, come alive! I mean the horse round-up. How we're going to keep that bunch uh skeletons under us all summer is a guessing contest for fair. Wooden Shoes has got t' give me about forty, instead of a dozen, if he wants me t' hit 'er up on circle the way I'm used to. I bet their back-bones'll wear clean up through our saddles."

"Oh, I guess not," said Rowdy calmly. "They ain't so thin—and they'll pick up flesh. There's some mighty good ones in the bunch, too. I hope Wooden Shoes don't forget to give me the first pick. There's one I got my eye on— that blue roan. Anyway, I guess you can wiggle along with less than forty."

Pink shook his head thoughtfully and sighed. Pink loved good mounts, and the outlook did not please him. The round-up had camped, for the last time, on the river within easy riding distance of Camas. The next day's drive would bring them to the home ranch, where Eagle Creek was fuming over the lateness of the season, the condition of the range, and the June rains, which had thus far failed even to moisten decently the grass-roots.

"Let's ride over to Camas; all the other fellows have gone," Pink proposed listlessly, drawing in his line.

Rowdy as listlessly consented. Camas as a town was neither interesting nor important; but when one has spent three long weeks communing with nature in her sulkiest and most unamiable mood, even a town without a railroad to its name may serve to relieve the monotony of living.

The sun was piling gorgeous masses of purple and crimson clouds high about him, cuddling his fat cheeks against their soft folds till, a Midas, he turned them to gold at the touch. Those farther away gloomed jealously at the favoritism of their lord, and huddled closer together—the purple for rage, perhaps; and the crimson for shame!

Pink's face was tinged daintily with the glow, and even Rowdy's lean, brown features were for the moment glorified. They rode knee to knee silently, thinking each his own thoughts the while they watched the sunset with eyes grown familiar with its barbaric splendor, but never indifferent.

Soon the west held none but the deeper tints, and the shadows climbed, with the stealthy tread of trailing Indians, from the valley, chasing the after-glow to the very hilltops, where it stood a moment at bay and then surrendered meekly to the dusk. A meadow-lark near-by cut the silence into haunting ripples of melody, stopped affrighted at their coming, and flew off into the dull glow of the west; his little body showed black against a crimson cloud. Out across the river a lone coyote yapped sharply, then trailed off into the weird plaint of his kind.

"Brother-in-law's in town to-day; Bob Nevin saw him," Pink remarked, when the coyote ceased wailing and held his peace.

"Who?" Rowdy only half-heard.

"Bob Nevin," repeated Pink naively.

"Don't get funny. Who did Bob see?"

"Brother-in-law. Yours, not mine. Jessie's tin god. If he's there yet, I bid for an invite to the 'swatfest.' Or maybe"—a horrible possibility forced itself upon Pink—"maybe you'll kill the fattest maverick and fall on his neck—"

"The maverick's?" Rowdy's brows were rather pinched together, but his tone told nothing.

"Naw; Harry Conroy's a fellow's liable to do most any fool thing when he's got schoolma'amitis."

"That so?"

Pink snorted. The possibility had grown to black certainty in his mind. He became suddenly furious.

"Lord! I hope some kind friend'll lead me out an' knock me in the head, if ever I get locoed over any darned girl!"

"Same here," agreed Rowdy, unmoved.

"Then your days are sure numbered in words uh one syllable, old-timer," snapped Pink.

Rowdy leaned and patted him caressingly upon the shoulder—a form of irony which Pink detested. "Don't get excited, sonny," he soothed. "Did you fetch your gun?"

"I sure did!" Pink drew a long breath of relief. "Yuh needn't think I'm going t' take chances on being no human colander. I've packed a gun for Harry Conroy ever since that rough-riding contest uh yourn. Yuh mind the way I took him under the ear with a rock? He's been makin' war-talk behind m' back ever since. Did I bring m' gun! Well, I guess yes!" He dimpled distractingly.

"All the same, it'll suit me not to run up against him," said Rowdy quite frankly. He knew Pink would understand. Then he lifted his coat suggestively, to show the weapon concealed beneath, and smiled.

"Different here. Yuh did have sense enough t' be ready—and if yuh see him, and don't forget he's got a sister with a number two foot, damned if I don't fix yuh both a-plenty!" He settled his hat more firmly over his curls, and eyed Rowdy anxiously from under his lashes.

Rowdy caught the action and the look from the tail of his eye, and grinned at his horse's ears. Pink in warlike mood always made him think of a four-year-old child playing pirate with the difference that Pink was always in deadly earnest and would fight like a fiend.

For more reasons than one he hoped they would not meet Harry Conroy. Jessie was still in ignorance of his real attitude toward her brother, and Rowdy wanted nothing more than to keep her so. The trouble was that he was quite certain to forget everything but his grievances, if ever he came face to face with Harry. Also, Pink would always fight quicker for his friends than for himself, and he felt very tender toward Pink. So he hoped fervently that Harry Conroy had already ridden back whence he came, and there would be no unpleasantness.

Four or five Cross L horses stood meekly before the Come Again Saloon, so Rowdy and Pink added theirs to the gathering and went in. The Silent One looked up from his place at a round table in a far corner, and beckoned.

"We need another hand here," he said, when they went over to him. "These gentlemen are worried because they might be taken into high society some day, and they would be placed in a very embarrassing position through their ignorance of bridge-whist. I have very magnanimously consented to teach them the rudiments."

Bob Nevin looked up, and then lowered an eyelid cautiously. "He's a liar. He offered to learn us how to play it; we bet him the drinks he didn't savvy the game himself. Set down, Pink, and I'll have you for my pretty pardner."

The Silent One shuffled the cards thoughtfully. "To make it seem like bona-fide bridge," he began, "we should have everybody playing."

"Aw, the common, ordinary brand is good enough," protested Bob. "I ain't in on any trimmings."

The Silent One smiled ever so slightly. "We should have prizes—or favors. Is there a store in town where one could buy something suitable?"

"They got codfish up here; I smelt it," suggested Jim Ellis. Him the Silent One ignored.

"What do you say, boys, to a real, high society whist-party? I'll invite the crowd, and be the hostess. And I'll serve punch—"

"Come on, fellows, and have one with me," called a strange voice near the door.

"Meeting's adjourned," cried Jim Ellis, and got up to accept the invitation and range along the bar with the rest. He had not been particularly interested in bridge-whist anyway.

The others remained seated, and the bartender called across to know what they would have. Pink cut the cards very carefully, and did not look up. Rowdy thrust both hands in his pockets and turned his square shoulder to the bar. He did not need to look—he knew that voice, with its shoddy heartiness.

Men began to observe his attitude, and looked at one another. When one is asked to drink with another, he must comply or decline graciously, if he would not give a direct insult.

Harry Conroy took three long steps and laid a hand on Rowdy's shoulder—a hand which Rowdy shook off as though it burned. "Say, stranger, are you too high-toned t' drink with a common cowpuncher?" he demanded sharply.

Rowdy half-turned toward him. "No, sir. But I'll be mighty thirsty before I drink with you." His voice was even, but it cut.

The room stilled on the instant; it was as if every man of them had turned to lay figures. Harry Conroy had winced at sight of Rowdy's face—men saw that, and some of them wondered. Pink leaned back in his chair, every nerve tightened for the next move, and waited. It was Harry—handsome, sneering, a certain swaggering defiance in his pose—who first spoke.

"Oh, it's you, is it? I haven't saw yuh for some time. How's bronco-fighting? Gone up against any more contests?" He laughed mockingly—with mouth and eyes maddeningly like Jessie's in teasing mood.

Rowdy could have killed him for the resemblance alone. His lids drooped sleepily over eyes that glittered. Harry saw the sign, read it for danger; but he laughed again.

"Yuh ought to have seen this bronco-peeler pull leather, boys," he jeered recklessly "I like to 'a' died. He got piled up the slickest I ever saw; and there was some feeble-minded Canucks had money up on him, too: He won't drink with me, 'cause I got off with the purse. He's got a grouch—and I don't know as I blame him; he did get let down pretty hard, for a fact."

"Maybe he did pull leather—but he didn't cut none, like you did, you damn' skunk!" It was Pink—Pink, with big, long-lashed eyes purple with rage, and with a dead-white streak around his mouth, and a gun in his hand.

Harry wheeled toward him, and if a new light of fear crept into his eyes, his lips belied it in a sneer. "Two of a kind!" he laughed. "So that's the story yuh brought over here, is it? Hell of a lot uh good it'll do yuh!"

Something in Pink's face warned Rowdy. Harry's face turned watchfully from one to the other. Evidently he considered Pink the more uncertain of the two; and he was quite justified in so thinking. Pink was only waiting for a cue before using his gun; and when Pink once began, there was no telling where or when he would leave off.

While Harry stood uncertain, Rowdy's fist suddenly spatted against his cheek with considerable force. He tumbled, a cursing heap, against the foot-rail of the bar, scrambled up like a cat—a particularly vicious cat—and came at Rowdy murderously. The Come Again would shortly have been filled with the pungent haze of burned powder, only that the bartender was a man-of-action. He hated brawls, and it did not matter to him how just might be the quarrel; he slapped the gaping barrels of a sawed-off shotgun across the bar—and from the look of it one might imagine many disagreeable things.

"Drop it! Cut it out!" he bellowed. "Yuh ain't going t' make no slaughter-pen out uh this joint, I tell yuh. Put up them guns or else take 'em outside. If you fellers are hell-bent on smokin' each other up, they's all kinds uh room outdoors. Git! Vamose! Hike!"

Conroy wheeled and walked, straight-backed and venomous, to the door. "Come on out, if yuh ain't scared," he sneered. "It's two agin' one and then some, by the look uh things. But I'll take yuh singly or in bunches. I'm ready for the whole damn' Cross L bunch uh coyotes. Come on, you white-livered—!"

Rowdy rushed for him, with Pink and the Silent One at his heels. He had forgotten that Harry Conroy ever had a sister of any sort whatsoever. All he knew was that Harry had done him much wrong, of the sort which comes near to being unforgivable, and that he had sneered insults that no man may overlook. All he thought of was to get his hands on him.

Outside, the dusky stillness made all sounds seem out of place; the faint starlight made all objects black and unfamiliar. Rowdy stopped, just off the threshold, blinking at the darkness which held his enemy. It was strange that he did not find him at his elbow, he thought—and a suspicion came to him that Harry was lying in wait; it would be like him. He stepped out of the yellow glare from a window and stood in more friendly shade. Behind him, on the door-step, stood the other two, blinking as he had done.

A form which he did not recognize rushed up out of the darkness and confronted the three belligerently. "You're a-disturbin' the peace," he yelled. "We don't stand for nothing like that in Camas. You're my prisoners—all uh yuh." The edict seemed to include even the bartender, peering over the shoulder of Bob Nevin, who struggled with several others for immediate passage through the doorway.

"I guess not, pardner," retorted Pink, facing him as defiantly as though the marshal were not twice his size.

The marshal lunged for him; but the Silent One, reaching a long arm from the door-step, rapped him smartly on the head with his gun. The marshal squawked and went down in a formless heap.

"Come on, boys," said the Silent One coolly. "I think we'd better go. Your friend seems to have vanished in thin air."

Rowdy, grumbling mightily over what looked unpleasantly like retreat, was pushed toward his horse and mounted under protest. Likewise Pink, who was for staying and cleaning up the whole town. But the Silent One was firm, and there was that in his manner which compelled obedience.

Harry Conroy might have been an optical—and aural—illusion, for all the trace there was of him. But when the three rode out into the little street, a bullet pinged close to Rowdy's left ear, and the red bark of a revolver spat viciously from a black shadow beside the Come Again.

Rowdy and the two turned and rode back, shooting blindly at the place, but the shadow yawned silently before them and gave no sign. Then the Silent One, observing that the marshal was getting upon a pair of very unsteady legs, again assumed the leadership, and fairly forced Rowdy and Pink into the homeward trail.

CHAPTER 7.
Rowdy in a Tough Place.

Rowdy, with nice calculation, met Miss Conroy just as she had left the school-house, and noted with much satisfaction that she was riding alone. Miss Conroy, if she had been at all observant, must have seen the light of some fixed purpose shining in his eyes; for Rowdy was resolved to make her a partner in his dreams of matters domestic. And, of a truth, his easy assurance was the thinnest of cloaks to hide his inner agitation.

"The round-up just got in yesterday afternoon," he told her, as he swung into the trail beside her. "We're going to start out again to-morrow, so this is about the only chance I'll have to see you for a while."

"I knew the round-up must be in," said Miss Conroy calmly. "I heard that you were in Camas a night or two ago."

Inwardly, Rowdy dodged. "We camped close to Camas," he conceded guardedly. "A lot of us fellows rode into town."

"Yes, so Harry told me," she said. "He came over to see me yesterday. He is going to leave—has already, in fact. He has had a fine position offered him by the Indian agent at Belknap. The agent used to be a friend of father's." She looked at Rowdy sidelong, and then went straight at what was in the minds of both.

"I'm sorry to hear, Mr. Vaughan, that you are on bad terms with Harry. What was the trouble?" She turned her head and smiled at him—but the smile did not bring his lips to answer; it was unpleasantly like the way Harry smiled when he had some deviltry in mind.

Rowdy scented trouble and parried. "Men can't always get along agreeably together."

"And you disagree with a man rather emphatically, I should judge. Harry said you knocked him down." Politeness ruled her voice, but cheeks and eyes were aflame.

"I did. And of course he told you how he took a shot at me from a dark corner, outside." Rowdy's eyes, it would seem, had kindled from the fire in hers.

"No, he didn't—but I—you struck him first."

"Hitting a man with your fist is one thing," said Rowdy with decision. "Shooting at him from ambush is another."

"Harry shouldn't have done that," she admitted with dignity. "But why wouldn't you take a drink with him? Not that I approve of drinking—I wish Harry wouldn't do such things—but he said it was an insult the way you refused."

"Jessie—"

"Miss Conroy, please."

"Jessie"—he repeated the name stubbornly—"I think we'd better drop that subject. You don't understand the case; and, anyway, I didn't come here to discuss Harry. Our trouble is long standing, and if I insulted him you ought to know I had a reason. I never came whining to you about him, and it don't speak well for him that he hot-footed over to you with his version. I suppose he'd heard about me—er—going to see you, and wanted to queer me. I hope you'll take my word for it, Jessie, that I've never harmed him; all the trouble he's made for himself, one way and another.

"But what I came over for to-day concerns just you and me. I wanted to tell you that—to ask you if you'll marry me. I might put it more artistic, Jessie, but that's what I mean, and—I mean all the things I'd like to say and can't." He stopped and smiled at her, wistfully whimsical. "I've been three weeks getting my feelings into proper words, little girl, and coming over here I had a speech thought out that sure done justice to my subject. But all I can remember of it is just that—that I want you for always."

Miss Conroy looked away from him, but he could see a deeper tint of red in her cheek. It seemed a long time before she said anything. Then: "But you've forgotten about Harry. He's my brother, and he'd be—er—you wouldn't want him related—to you."

"Harry! Well, I pass him up. I've got a pretty long account against him; but I'll cross it off. It won't be hard to do—for you. I've thought of all that; and a man can forgive a whole lot in the brother of the woman he loves." He leaned toward her and added honestly: "I can't promise you I'll ever get to like him, Jessie; but I'll keep my hands off him, and I'll treat him civil; and when you consider all he's done, that's quite a large-sized contract."

Miss Conroy became much interested in the ears of her horse.

"The only thing to decide is whether you like me enough. If you do, we'll sure be happy. Never mind Harry."

"You're very generous," she flared, "telling me to never mind Harry. And Harry's my own brother, and the only near relative I've got. I know he's—impulsive, and quick-tempered, perhaps. But he needs me all the more. Do you think I'll turn against him, even for you?"

That "even" may have been a slip, but it heartened Rowdy immensely. "I don't ask you to," he told her gently. "I only want you to not turn against me."

"I do wish you two would be sensible, and stop quarreling." She glanced at him briefly.

"I'm willing to cut it out—I told you that. I can't answer for him, though." Rowdy sighed, wishing Harry Conroy in Australia, or some place equally remote.

Miss Conroy suddenly resolved to be strictly just; and when a young woman sets about being deliberately just, the Lord pity him whom she judges!

"Before I answer you, I must know just what all this is about," she said firmly. "I want to hear both sides; I'm sure Harry wouldn't do anything mean. Do you think he would?"

Rowdy was dissentingly silent.

"Do you really, in your heart, believe that Harry would—knowingly—be guilty of anything mean?" Her eyes plainly told the answer she wanted to hear.

Rowdy looked into them, hesitated, and clung tenaciously to his convictions. "Yes, I do; and I know Harry pretty well, Jessie." His face showed how much he hated to say it.

"I'm afraid you are very prejudiced," she sighed. "But go on; tell me just what you have against Harry. I'm sure it can all be explained away, only I must hear what it is."

Rowdy regarded her, puzzled. How he was to comply he did not know. It would be simply brutal to tell her. He would feel like a hangman. And she believed so in Harry, she wouldn't listen; even if she did, he thought bitterly, she would hate him for destroying her faith. A woman's justice—ah, me!

"Don't you see you're putting me in a mighty hard position, girlie?" he protested. "You're a heap better off not to know. He's your brother. I wish you'd take my word that I'll drop the whole thing right where it is. Harry's had all the best of it, so far; let it stand that way."

Her eyes met his coldly. "Are you afraid to let me judge between you? What did he do? Daren't you tell?"

Rowdy's lids drooped ominously. "If you call that a dare," he said grimly, "I'll tell you, fast enough. I was a friend to him when he needed one mighty bad. I helped him when he was dead broke and out uh work. I kept him going all winter—and to show his gratitude, he gave me the doublecross, in more ways than one. I won't go into details." He decided that he simply could not tell her bluntly that Harry had worked off stolen horses on him, and worse.

"Oh—you won't go into details!" Scorn filled eyes and voice. "Are they so trivial, then? You tell me what you did for Harry—playing Good Samaritan. Harry, let me tell you, has property of his own; I can't see why he should ever be in need of charity. You're like all the rest; you hint things against him—but I believe it's just jealousy. You can't come out honestly and tell me a single instance where he has harmed you, or done anything worse than other high-spirited young men."

"It wouldn't do any good to tell you," he retorted. "You think he's just lacking wings to be an angel. I hope to God you'll always be able to think so! I'm sure I don't want to jar your faith."

"I must say your actions don't bear out your words. You've just been trying to turn me against him."

"I haven't. I've been trying to convince you that I want you, anyway, and Harry needn't come between us."

"In other words, you're willing to overlook my being Harry's sister. I appreciate your generosity, I'm sure." She did not look, however, as if she meant that.

"I didn't mean that."

"Then you won't overlook it? How very unfortunate! Because I can't help the relationship."

"Would you, if you could?" he asked rashly.

"Certainly not!"

"I'm afraid we're getting off the trail," he amended tactfully. "I asked you, a while back, if you'd marry me."

"And I said I must hear both sides of your trouble with Harry, before I could answer."

"What's the use? You'd take his part, anyway."

"Not if I found he was guilty of all you—insinuate. I should be perfectly just." She really believed that.

"Can't you tell me yes or no, anyway? Don't let him come between us."

"I can't help it. We'd never agree, or be happy. He'd keep on coming between us, whether we meant him to or not," she said dispiritedly.

"That's a cinch," Rowdy muttered, thinking of Harry's trouble-breeding talents.

"Then there's no more to be said. Until you and Harry settle your difficulties amicably, or I am convinced that he's in the wrong, we'll just be friends, Mr. Vaughan. Good afternoon." She rode into the Rodway yard, feeling very just and virtuous, no doubt. But she left Rowdy with some rather unpleasant thoughts, and with a sentiment toward her precious brother which was not far from manslaughter.

CHAPTER 8.
Pink in a Threatening Mood.

Eagle Creek Smith had at last reached the point where he must face new conditions and change established customs. He could no longer ignore the barrenness of the range, or close his eyes to the grim fact that his cattle were facing starvation—and that in June, when they should be taking on flesh.

When he finally did confess to himself that things couldn't go on like that, others had been before him in leasing and buying land, until only the dry benches were left to him and his hungry herds.

But Eagle Creek was a man of resource. When the round-up pulled in and Wooden Shoes reported to him the general state of the cattle, and told of the water-holes newly fenced and of creek bottoms gobbled by men more farseeing than he, Eagle Creek took twenty-four hours to adjust himself to the situation and to meet the crisis before him. His own land, as compared to his twenty thousand cattle, was too pitifully inadequate for a second thought.

He must look elsewhere for the correct answer to his problem.

When Rowdy rode apathetically up to the stable, Pink came out of the bunk-house to meet him, big with news. "Oh, doctor! We're up against it a-plenty now," he greeted, with his dimples at their deepest.

"Huh!" grunted Rowdy crossly. "What's hurting you, Pink?"

"Forecasting the future," Pink retorted. "Eagle Creek has come alive, and has wised up sudden to the fact that this ain't going t' be any Noah's flood brand uh summer, and that his cattle look like the tailings of a wash-board factory. He's got busy—and we're sure going to. We're due t' hit the grit out uh here in the first beams uh rosy morn, and do a record stunt at gathering cattle."

"Well, we were going to, anyhow," Rowdy cut in.

"But that's only the prelude, old-timer. We've got t' take 'em across country to the Belknap reservation. Eagle Creek went t' town and telegraphed, and got the refusal of it for pasturage; he ain't so slow, oncet he gets started. But if you've ever rode over them dried-up benches, you savvy the merry party we'll be when we git there. I've saw jack-rabbits packing their lunch along over there."

"Belknap"—Rowdy dropped his saddle spitefully to the ground—"is where our friend Conroy has just gone to fill a splendid position."

Pink thoughtfully blew the ashes from his cigarette. "Harry Conroy would fill one position fine. So one uh these days I'll offer it to him. I don't know anybody that'd look nicer in a coffin than that jasper—and if he's gone t' Belknap, that's likely the position he'll fill, all right."

Rowdy said nothing, but his very silence told Pink much.

"How'd yuh make out with Jessie?" Pink asked frankly, though he was not supposed to know where Rowdy had been.

Rowdy knew from experience that it was useless trying to keep anything from Pink that Pink wanted to know; besides, there was a certain comfort in telling his troubles to so stanch a friend. "Harry got his work in there, too," he said bitterly. "He beat me to her and queered me for good, by the looks."

"Huh!" said Pink. "I wouldn't waste much time worrying over her, if she's that easy turned."

"She's all right," defended Rowdy quickly. "I don't know as I blame her; she takes the stand any sister would take. She wants to know all about the trouble—hear both sides, she said, so she could judge which was to blame. I guess she's got her heart set on being peacemaker. I know one thing: she— likes me, all right."

"I don't see how he queered yuh any, then," puzzled Pink. "She sure couldn't take his part after you'd told her all he done."

Rowdy turned on him savagely. "You little fool, do you think I told her? Right there's the trouble. He told his story; and when she asked for mine, I couldn't say anything. She's his sister."

"You—didn't—tell!" Pink leaned against the stable and stared. "Rowdy Vaughan, there's times when even your friend can't disguise the fact that yuh act plumb batty. Yuh let Harry do yuh dirt that any other man'd 'a' killed him on bare suspicion uh doing; and yuh never told her when she asked yuh to! How yuh lent him money, and let him steal some right out uh your pocket—"

"I couldn't prove that," Rowdy objected.

"And yuh never told her about his cutting your latigo—"

"Oh, cut it out!" Rowdy glowered down at him. "I guess I don't need to be reminded of all those things. But are they the things a man can tell a girl about her brother? Pink, you're about as unfeeling a little devil as I ever run across. Maybe you'd have told her; but I couldn't. So it's all off."

He turned away and stared unseeingly at the rim of hills that hid the place where she lived. She seemed very far away from him just then—and very,

very desirable. He thought then that he had never before realized just how much he cared.

"You can jest bet I'd 'a' told her!" gritted Pink, watching furtively Rowdy's averted face. "She ain't goin' t' be bowed down by no load of ignorance much longer, either. If she don't get Harry Conroy's pedigree straight out, without the varnish, it'll be because I ain't next to all his past."

But Rowdy, glooming among the debris of certain pet air-castles, neither heard nor wanted to hear Pink's wrathful mutterings. As a matter of fact, it was not till Pink clattered out of the yard on Mascot that he remembered where he was. Even then it did not occur to him to wonder where Pink was going.

CHAPTER 9.
Moving the Herd.

Four thousand weary cattle crawled up the long ridge which divides Chin Coulee from Quitter Creek. Pink, riding point, opposite the Silent One, twisted round in his saddle and looked back at the slow-moving river of horns and backs veiled in a gray dust-cloud. Down the line at intervals rode the others, humped listlessly in their saddles, their hat brims pulled low over tired eyes that smarted with dust and wind and burning heat.

Pink sighed, and wished lonesomely that it was Rowdy riding point with him, instead of the Silent One, who grew even more silent as the day dragged leadenly to mid-afternoon; Pink could endure anything better than being left to his thoughts and to the complaining herd for company.

He took off his hat, pushed back his curls—dripping wet they were and flattened unbecomingly in pasty, yellow rings on his forehead—and eyed with disfavor a line-backed, dry cow, with one horn tipped rakishly toward her speckled nose; she blinked silently at wind and heat, and forged steadily ahead, up-hill and down coulee, always in the lead, always walking, walking, like an automaton. Her energy, in the face of all the dry, dreary days, rasped Pink's nerves unbearably. For nearly a week he had ridden left point, and always that line-backed cow with the down-crumpled horn walked and walked and walked, a length ahead of her most intrepid followers.

He leaned from his saddle, picked up a rock from the barren, yellow hillside, and threw it at the cow spitefully. The rock bounced off her lean rump; she blinked and broke into a shuffling trot, her dragging hoofs kicking up an extra amount of dust, which blew straight into Pink's face.

"Aw, cut it out!" he shouted petulantly. "You're sure the limit, without doing any stunts at sprinting up-hill. Ain't yuh got any nerves, yuh blamed old skate? Yuh act like it was milkin'-time, and yuh was headed straight for the bars and a bran mash. Can't yuh realize the kind uh deal you're up against? Here's cattle that's got you skinned for looks, old girl, and they know it's coming blamed tough; and you just bat your eyes and peg along like yuh enjoyed it. Bawl, or something, can't yuh? Drop back a foot and act human!"

The Silent One looked across at him with a tired smile. "Let her go, Pink, and pray for more like her," he called amusedly. "There'll be enough of them dropping back presently."

Pink threw one leg over the horn and rode sidewise, made him a cigarette, and tried to forget the cow—or, at least, to forgive her for not acting as dog-tired as he felt.

They were on the very peak of the ridge now, and the hill sloped smoothly down before them to the bluff which bounded Quitter Creek. Far down, a tiny black speck in the coulee-bottom, they could see Wooden Shoes riding along the creek-bank, scouting for water. From the way he rode, and from the fact that camp was nowhere in sight, Pink guessed shrewdly that his quest was in vain. He shrugged his shoulders at what that meant, and gave his attention to the herd.

The marching line split at the brow of the bluff. The line-backed cow lowered her head a bit and went unfaltering down the parched, gravel-coated hill, followed by a few hundred of the freshest. Then the stream stopped flowing, and Pink and the Silent One rode back up the bluff to where the bulk of the footsore herd, their senses dulled by hunger and weariness and choking thirst, sniffed at the gravel that promised agony to their bruised feet, and balked at the ordeal. Others straggled up, bunched against the rebels, and stood stolidly where they were.

Pink galloped on down the crawling line. "Forward, the Standard Oil Brigade!" he yelled whimsically as he went.

The cowboys heard—and understood. They left their places and went forward at a lope, and Pink rode back to the coulee edge, untying his slicker as he went. The Silent One was already off his horse and shouting hoarsely as he whacked with his slicker at the sulky mass. Pink rode in and did the same. It was not the first time this thing had happened, and from a diversion it was verging closely on the monotonous. Presently, even a rank tenderfoot must have caught the significance of Pink's military expression. The Standard Oil Brigade was at the front in force.

Cowboys, swinging five-gallon oil-cans, picked up from scattered sheep camps and carried many a weary mile for just such an emergency, were charging the bunch intrepidly. Others made shift with flat sirup-cans with pebbles inside. A few, like Pink and the Silent One, flapped their slickers till their arms ached. Anything, everything that would make a din and startle the cattle out of their lethargy, was pressed into service.

But they might have been raised in a barnyard and fed cabbage leaves from back door-steps, for all the excitement they showed. Cattle that three months ago—or a month—would run, head and tail high in air, at sight of a man on foot, backed away from a rattling, banging cube of gleaming tin, turned and faced the thing dull-eyed and apathetic.

In time, however, they gave way dogedly before the onslaught. A few were forced shrinkingly down the hill; others followed gingerly, until the line lengthened and flowed, a sluggish, brown-red stream, into the coulee and across to Quitter Creek.

Here the leaders were browsing greedily along the banks. They had emptied the few holes that had still held a meager store of brackish water and so the mutinous bulk of the herd snuffed at the trampled, muddy spots and bellowed their disappointment.

Wooden Shoes rode up and surveyed the half maddened animals gloomily. "Push 'em on, boys," he said. "They's nothings for 'em here. I've sent the wagons on to Red Willow; we'll try that next. Push 'em along all yuh can, while I go on ahead and see."

With tin-cans, slickers, and much vituperation, they forced the herd up the coulee side and strung them out again on trail. The line-backed cow walked and walked in the lead before Pink's querulous gaze, and the others plodded listlessly after. The gray dust-cloud formed anew over their slowmoving backs, and the cowboys humped over in their saddles and rode and rode, with the hot sun beating aslant in their dirt-grimed faces, and with the wind blowing and blowing.

If this had been the first herd to make that dreary trip, things would not have been quite so disheartening. But it was the third. Seven thousand lean kine had passed that way before them, eating the scant grass growth and drinking what water they could find among those barren, sun-baked coulees.

The Cross L boys, on this third trip, were become a jaded lot of hollow-eyed men, whose nerves were rasped raw with long hours and longer days in the saddle. Pink's cheeks no longer made his name appropriate, and he was not the only one who grew fretful over small things. Rowdy had been heard, more than once lately, to anathematize viciously the prairie-dogs for standing on their tails and chipchip-chipping at them as they went by. And though the Silent One did not swear, he carried rocks in his pockets, and threw them with venomous precision at every "dog" that showed his impertinent nose out of a burrow within range. For Pink, he vented his spleen on the line-backed cow.

So they walked and walked and walked.

The cattle balked at another hill, and all the tincans and slickers in the crowd could scarcely move them. The wind dropped with the sun, and the clouds glowed gorgeously above them, getting scant notice, except that they told eloquently of the coming night; and there were yet miles—long, rough, heartbreaking miles—to put behind them before they could hope for the things their tired bodies craved: supper and dreamless sleep.

When the last of the herd had sidled, under protest, down the long hill to the flat, dusk was pushing the horizon closer upon them, mile by mile. When they crawled sinuously out upon the welcome level, the hill loomed ghostly and black behind them. A mile out, Wooden Shoes rode out of the gloom and met the point. He turned and rode beside Pink.

"Yuh'll have t' swing 'em north," he greeted.

"Red Willow's dry as hell—all but in the Rockin' R field. No use askin' ole Mullen to let us in there; we'll just go. I sent the wagons through the fence, an' yuh'll find camp about a mile up from the mouth uh the big coulee. You swing 'em round the end uh this bench, an' hit that big coulee at the head. When you come t' the fence, tear it down. They's awful good grass in that field!"

"All right," said Pink cheerfully. It was in open defiance of range etiquette; but their need was desperate. The only thing about it Pink did not like was the long detour they must make. He called the news across to the Silent One, after Wooden Shoes had gone on down the line, and they swung the point gradually to the left.

Before that drive was over, Pink had vowed many times to leave the range forever and never to turn another cow—besides a good many other foolish things which would be forgotten, once he had a good sleep. And Rowdy, plodding half-way down the herd, had grown exceedingly pessimistic regarding Jessie Conroy, and decided that there was no sense in thinking about her all the time, the way he had been doing. Also, he told himself savagely that if Harry ever crossed his trail again, there would be something doing. This thing of letting a cur like that run roughshod over a man on account of a girl that didn't care was plumb idiotic. And beside him the cattle walked and walked and walked, a dim, moving mass in the quiet July night.

CHAPTER 10.
Harry Conroy at Home.

It was late next morning when they got under way; for they had not reached camp until long after midnight, and Wooden Shoes was determined the cattle should have one good feed, and all the water they wanted, to requite them for the hard drive of the day before.

Pink rode out with Rowdy to the herd—a heavylidded, gloomy Rowdy he was, and not amiably inclined toward the small talk of the range. But Pink had slept five whole hours and was almost his normal self; which means that speech was not to be denied him.

"What yuh mourning over?" he bantered. "Mad 'cause the reservation's so close?"

"Sure," assented Rowdy, with deep sarcasm.

"That's what I thought. Studying up the nicest way uh giving brother-in-law the glad hand, ain't yuh?"

"He's no relation uh mine—and never will be," said Rowdy curtly. "And I'll thank you, Pink, to drop that subject for good and all."

"Down she goes," assented Pink, quite unperturbed. "But the cards ain't all turned yet, yuh want to remember, I wouldn't pass on no hand like you've got. If I wanted a girl right bad, Rowdy, I'd wait till I got refused before I'd quit."

"Seems to me you've changed your politics lately," Rowdy retorted. "A while back you was cussing the whole business; and now you're worse than an old maid aunt. Pink, you may not be wise to the fact, but you sure are an inconsistent little devil."

"Are yuh going t' hunt Harry up and—"

"I thought I told you to drop that."

"Did yuh? All right, then—only I hope yuh didn't leave your gun packed away in your bed," he insinuated.

"You can take a look to-night, if you want to."

Pink laughed in a particularly infectious way he had, and, before he quite knew it, Rowdy was laughing, also. After that the world did not look quite so forlorn as it had, nor the day's work so distasteful. So Pink, having accomplished his purpose, was content to turn the subject.

"There's old Liney"—he pointed her out to Rowdy—"fresh as a meadow-lark. I had a big grouch against her yesterday, just because she batted her eyes and kept putting one foot ahead uh the other. I could 'a' killed her. But she's all right, that old girl. The way she led out down that black coulee last night wasn't slow! Say, she's an ambitious old party. I wish you was riding point with me, Rowdy. The Silent One talks just about as much as that old cow. He sure loves to live up to his rep."

"Oh, go on to work," Rowdy admonished. "You make me think of a magpie." All the same, he looked after him with smiling lips, and eyes that forgot their gloom. He even whistled while he helped round up the scattered herd, ready for that last day's drive.

Every man in the outfit comforted himself with the thought that it was the last day's drive. After long weeks of trailing lean herds over barren, windbrushed hills, the last day meant much to them. Even the Silent One sang something they had never heard before, about "If Only I Knew You Were True."

They crossed the Rocking R field, took down four panels of fence, passed out, and carefully put them up again behind them. Before them stretched level plain for two miles; beyond that a high, rocky ridge that promised some trouble with the herd, and after that more plain and a couleee or two, and then, on a far slope—the reservation.

The cattle were rested and fed, and walked out briskly; the ridge neared perceptibly. Pink's shrill whistle carried far back down the line and mingled pleasantly with voices calling to one another across the herd. Not a man was humped listlessly in his saddle; instead, they rode with shoulders back and hats at divers jaunty angles to keep the sun from shining in eyes that faced the future cheerfully.

The herd steadily climbed the ridge, choosing the smoothest path and the easiest slope. Pink assured the line-backed cow that she was a peach, and told her to "go to it, old girl." The Silent One's pockets were quite empty of rocks, and the prairiedogs chipped and flirted their funny little tails unassailed. And Rowdy, from wondering what had made Pink change his attitude so abruptly, began to plan industriously the next meeting with Jessie Conroy, and to build a new castle that was higher and airier than any he had ever before attempted—and perhaps had a more flimsy foundation; for it rested precariously on Pink's idle remarks.

The point gained the top of the ridge, and Pink turned and swung his hat jubilantly at the others. The reservation was in sight, though it lay several miles distant. But in that clear air one could distinguish the line fence—if one had the eye of faith and knew just where to look. Presently he observed a familiar horseman climbing the ridge to meet them.

"Eagle Creek's coming," he shouted to the man behind. "Come alive, there, and don't let 'em roam all over the map. Git some style on yuh!"

Those who heard laughed; no one ever dreamed of being offended at what Pink said. Those who had not heard had the news passed on to them, in various forms. Wooden Shoes, who had been loitering in the rear gossiping with the men, rode on to meet Smith.

Eagle Creek urged his horse up the last steep place, right in the face of the leaders, which halted and tried to turn back. Pink, swearing in a whisper, began to force them forward.

"Let 'em alone," Eagle Creek bellowed harshly. "They ain't goin' no farther."

"W-what?" Pink stopped short and eyed him critically. Eagle Creek could not justly be called a teetotaler; but Pink had never known him to get worse than a bit wobbly in his legs; his mind had never fogged perceptibly. Still, something was wrong with him, that was certain. Pink glanced dubiously across at the Silent One and saw him shrug his shoulders expressively.

Eagle Creek rode up and stopped within ten feet of the line-backed cow; she seemed hurt at being held up in this manner, Pink thought.

"Yuh'll have t' turn this herd back," Eagle Creek announced bluntly.

"Where to?" Pink asked, too stunned to take in the meaning of it.

"T' hell, I guess. It's the only place I know of where everybody's welcome." Eagle Creek's tone was not pleasant.

"We just came from there," Pink said simply, thinking of the horrors of that drive.

"Where's Wooden Shoes?" snapped the old man; and the foreman's hat-crown appeared at that instant over the ridge.

"Well, we're up against it," Eagle Creek greeted. "That damn' agent—or the fellow he had workin' for him—reported his renting us pasture. Made the report read about twice as many as we're puttin' on. He's got orders now t' turn out every hoof but what b'longs there."

"My Lord!" Wooden Shoes gasped at the catastrophe which faced the Cross L.

"That's Harry Conroy's work," Pink cut in sharply' "He'd hurt the Cross L if he could, t' spite me and Rowdy. He—"

"Don't matter—seein' it's done. Yuh might as well turn the herd loose right here, an' let 'em go t' the devil. I don't know what else t' do with 'em."

"Anything gone wrong?" It was Rowdy, who had left his place and ridden forward to see what was holding the herd back.

"Naw. We're fired off the reservation, is all. We got orders to take the herd to hell. Eagle Creek's leased it. Mr. Satan is going to keep house here in Montana; he says it's better for his trade," Pink informed him, in his girlish treble.

Eagle Creek turned on him fiercely, then thought better of it and grinned. "Them arrangements wouldn't make us any worse off'n what we are," he commented. "Turn 'em loose, boys."

"Man, if yuh turn 'em loose here, the first storm that hits 'em, they all die," Wooden Shoes interposed excitedly. "They ain't nothings for 'em. We had t' turn 'em into the Rockin' R field last night, t' git water an' feed. Red Willow's gone dry outside dat field. They ain't—nothings. They'll die!"

Eagle Creek looked at him dully. For the first time in his life he faced utter ruin. "Damn 'em, let 'em die, then!" he said.

"That's what they'll sure do," Wooden Shoes reiterated stubbornly. "If they don't git feed and water now, yuh needn't start no round-up next spring."

Pink's eyes went down over the close-huddled backs and the thicket of polished horns, and his eyelids stung. Would all of them die, he wondered! Four thousand! He hoped not. There must be some way out. Down the hill, he knew the cowboys were making cigarettes while they waited and wondered mightily what it was all about If they only knew, he thought, there would be more than one rope ready for Harry Conroy.

"How about the Peck reservation? Couldn't you get them on there?" Rowdy ventured.

"Not a hoof!" growled Eagle Creek, with his chin sunk against his chest. "There's thirty thousand Valley County cattle on there now." He looked down at the cattle, as Pink had done. "God! It's bad enough t' go broke," he groaned; "but t' think uh them poor brutes dyin' off in bunches, for want uh grass an' water! I've run that brand fer over thirty year."

CHAPTER 11.
Rowdy Promoted.

Rowdy rode closer. "If you don't mind paying duty," he began tentatively, "I can put you next to a range over the line, where I'll guarantee feed and water the year round for every hoof you own."

Eagle Creek lifted his head and looked at him "Whereabouts?" he demanded skeptically.

"Up in the Red Deer country. Pink knows the place. There's range a-plenty, and creeks running through that never go dry; and the country isn't stocked and fenced to death, like this is."

"And would we be ordered off soon as we got there?"

"Sure not—if you paid duty, which would only be about double what you were going to pay for one year's pasture."

Eagle Creek breathed deeply, like a man who has narrowly escaped suffocation. "Young man, I b'lieve you're a square dealer, and that yuh savvy the cow business. I've thought it ever since yuh started t' work." His keen old eyes twinkled at the memory of Rowdy's arrival, and Rowdy grinned. "I take yuh at your word, and yuh can consider yourself in charge uh this herd as it stands. Take it t' that cow heaven yuh tell about—and damn it, yuh won't be none the worse for it!"

"We'll pass that up," said Rowdy quietly. "I'll take the herd through, though; and I'd advise you to get the rest on the road as soon as they can be gathered. It's a three-hundred-mile drive."

"All right. From now on it's up to you," Eagle Creek told him briskly. "Take 'em back t' the Rockin' R field, and I'll send the wagons back t' you. Old Mullen'll likely make a roar—but that's most all gove'ment land he's got fenced, so I guess I can calm him down. Will yuh go near the ranch?"

"I think so," said Rowdy. "It will be the shortest way."

"Well, I'll give yuh some blank checks, an' you can load up with grub and anything else yuh need. I'll be over there by the time you are, and fix up that duty business. Wooden Shoes'll have t' get another outfit together, and get another bunch on the trail. One good thing—I got thirty days t' get off what cattle is on there; and thirty days uh grass and water'll put 'em in good shape for the trip. Wish this bunch was as well fixed."

"That's what," Rowdy assented. "But I think they'll make it, all right."

"I'll likely want yuh to stay up there and keep cases on 'em. Any objections?"

"Sure not!" laughed Rowdy. "Only I'll want Pink and the Silent One to stay with me."

"Keep what men yuh want. Anything else?"

"I don't think of anything," said Rowdy. "Only I'd like to have a—talk—with Conroy." Creek eyed him sharply. "Yuh won't be apt t' meet him. Old Bill Brown, up home, would like to see him, too. Bill's a perseverin' old cuss, and wants to see Conroy so bad he's got the sheriff out lookin' for him. It's about a bunch uh horses that was run off, three years ago. Yuh brought one of 'em back into the country last spring, yuh mind."

Rowdy and Pink looked at one another, but said nothing.

"Old Bill, he follered your back trail and found out some things he wanted t' know. Conroy got wind of it, though, and he left the agency kind-a suddint. No use yuh lookin' for him."

"Then we're ready to hit the grit, I guess." Rowdy glanced again at Pink who nodded.

"Well, I ain't stoppin' yuh," Eagle Creek drawled laconically. "S'-long, and good luck t' yuh."

He waited while Pink and the Silent One swung the point back down the hill, with Rowdy helping them, quite unmoved by his sudden promotion. When the herd was fairly started on the backward march, Eagle Creek nodded satisfaction the while he pried off a corner of plug-tobacco.

"He's all right," he asserted emphatically. "That boy suits me, from the ground up. If he don't put that deal through in good shape, it'll be becaus' it can't be did."

Wooden Shoes, with whom Rowdy had always been a prime favorite, agreed with Dutch heartiness. Then, leaving the herd to its new guardian they rode swiftly to overtake and turn back the wagons.

"Three hundred miles! And part of it across howling desert!" Rowdy drew his brows together. "It's a big thing for me, all right, Pink; but it's sure a big contract to take this herd through, if anybody should happen to ask yuh."

"Oh, buck up! You'll make good, all right—if only these creeks wasn't so bone dry!"

"Well, there's water enough in the Rocking R field for to-day; we'll throw 'em in there till tomorrow. And I've a notion I can find a better trail across to North Fork than the way we came. I'm going to strike out this afternoon and see, anyway, if Quitter Creek hasn't got water farther up. Once we get up north uh the home ranch, I can see my way clear."

"Go to it, boss," Pink cried heartily. "I don't see how I'm goin t' keep from sassing yuh, once in a while, though. That's what bothers me. What'll happen if I turn loose on yuh, some time?"

"You'll get fired, I expect," laughed Rowdy, and rode off to announce the news to the rest of the outfit, who were very unhappy in their mystification.

If their reception of the change of plans and foreman was a bit profane, and their manner toward him a bit familiar, Rowdy didn't mind. He knew that they did not grudge him his good luck, even while they hated the long drive. He also knew that they watched him furtively; for nothing—not even misfortune—is as sure a test of a man's character as success. They liked Rowdy, and they did not believe this would spoil him; still, every man of them was secretly a bit anxious.

On the trail, he rode in his accustomed place, and, so far as appearances went, the party had no foreman. He went forward and helped Pink take down the fence that had been so carefully put up a few hours before, and he whistled while he put it in place again, just as if he had no responsibility in the world. Then the cattle were left to themselves, and the men rode down to their old campground, marked by empty tin-cans and a trodden place where had been the horse corral.

Rowdy swung down and faced the men gravely. Instinctively they stood at attention, waiting for what he had to say; they felt that the situation was so far out of the ordinary that a few remarks pertaining to their new relations would not be out of place.

He looked them over appraisingly, and met glances as grave as his own. Straight, capable fellows they were, every man of them.

"Boys," he began impressively, "you all know that from to-day on you're working under my orders. I never was boss of anything but the cayuse I happened to have under me, and I'm going to extract all the honey there is in the situation. Maybe I'll never be boss again—but at present I'm it. I want you fellows to remember that important fact, and treat me with proper respect. From now on you can call me Mr. Vaughan; 'Rowdy' doesn't go, except on a legal holiday.

"Furthermore, I'm not going to get out at daylight and catch up my own horse; I'll let yuh take turns being flunky, and I'll expect yuh to saddle my horse every morning and noon, and bring him to the cook-tent—and hold my stirrup for me. Also, you are expected, at all times and places, to anticipate my wants and fall over yourselves waiting on me. You're just common, ordinary, forty-dollar cow-punchers, and if I treat yuh white, it's because I pity yuh for not being up where I am. Remember, vassals, that I'm your superior, mentally, morally, socially—"

"Chap him!" yelled Pink, and made for him "I'll stand for a lot, but don't yuh ever think I'm a vassal!"

"Mutiny is strictly prohibited!" he thundered. "Villains, beware! Gadzooks—er—let's have a swim before the wagons come!"

They laughed and made for the creek, feeling rather crestfallen and a bit puzzled.

"If I had an outfit like this to run, and a three hundred-mile drive to make," Bob Nevin remarked to the Silent One, "blessed if I'd make a josh of it! I'd cultivate the corrugated brow and the stiff spine—me!"

"My friend," the Silent One responded, "don't be too hasty in your judgment. It's because the corrugated brow will come later that he laughs now. You'll presently find yourself accomplishing the impossible in obedience to the flicker of Rowdy Vaughan's eyelids. Man, did you never observe the set of his head, and the look of his eye? Rowdy Vaughan will get more out of this crowd than any man ever did; and if he fails, he'll fail with the band playing 'Hot Time.'"

"Maybe so," Bob admitted, not quite convinced; "but I wonder if he realizes what he's up against." At which the Silent One only smiled queerly as he splashed into the water.

After dinner Rowdy caught up the blue roan, which was his favorite for a hard ride—he seemed to have forgotten his speech concerning "flunkies"—and rode away up the coulee which had brought them into the field the night before. The boys watched him go, speculated a lot, and went to sleep as the best way of putting in the afternoon.

Pink, who knew quite well what was in Rowdy's mind, said nothing at all; it is possible that he was several degrees more jealous of the dignity of Rowdy's position than was Rowdy himself, who had no time to think of anything but the best way of getting the herd to Canada. He would like to have gone along, only that Rowdy did not ask him to. Pink assured himself that it was best for Rowdy not to start playing any favorites, and curled down in the bed-tent with the others and went to sleep.

It was late that night when Rowdy crept silently into his corner of the tent; but Pink was awake, and whispered to know if he found water. Rowdy's "Yes" was a mere breath, but it was enough.

At sunrise the herd trailed up the Rocking R coulee, and Pink and the Silent One pointed them north of the old trail.

CHAPTER 12.
"You Can Tell Jessie."

In the days that followed Rowdy was much alone. There was water to hunt, far ahead of the herd, together with the most practicable way of reaching it. He did not take the shortest way across that arid country and leave the next day's camping-place to chance—as Wooden Shoes had done. He felt that there was too much at stake, and the cattle were too thin for any more dry drives; long drives there were, but such was his generalship that there was always water at the end.

He rode miles and miles that he might have shirked, and he never slept until the next day's move, at least, was clearly defined in his mind and he felt sure that he could do no better by going another route.

These lonely rides gave him over to the clutch of thoughts he had never before harbored in his sunny nature. Grim, ugly thoughts they were, and not nice to remember afterward. They swung persistently around a central subject, as the earth revolves around the sun; and, like the earth, they turned and turned on the axis of his love for a woman.

In particularly ugly moods he thought that if Harry Conroy were caught and convicted of horsestealing, Jessie must perforce admit his guilt and general unworthiness—Rowdy called it general cussedness—and Rowdy be vindicated in her eyes. Then she would marry him, and go with him to the Red Deer country and—air-castles for miles! When he awoke to the argument again, he would tell himself savagely that if he could, by any means, bring about Conroy's speedy conviction, he would do so.

This was unlike Rowdy, whose generous charity toward his enemies came near being a fault. He might feel any amount of resentment for wrong done, but cold-blooded revenge was not in him; that he had suffered so much at Conroy's hands was due largely to the fact that Conroy was astute enough to read Rowdy aright, and unscrupulous enough to take advantage. Add to that a smallminded jealousy of Rowdy's popularity and horsemanship, one can easily imagine him doing some rather nasty things. Perhaps the meanest, and the one which rankled most in Rowdy's memory, was the cutting of Rowdy's latigo just before a riding contest, in which the purse and the glory of a championship-belt seemed in danger of going to Rowdy.

Rowdy had got a fall that crippled him for weeks, and Harry had won the purse and belt—and the enmity of several men better than he. For though morally sure of his guilt, no one could prove that he had cut the strap, and so he got off unpunished, except that Pink thrashed him—a bit unscientifically, it is true, since he resorted to throwing rocks toward the last, but with a thoroughness worthy even of Pink.

But in moods less ugly he shrank from the hurt that must be Jessie's if she should discover the truth. Jessie's brother a convicted thief serving his sentence in Deer Lodge! The thought was horrible; it was brutal cruelty. If he could only know where to look for that lad, he'd help him out of the country. It was no good shutting him up in jail; that wouldn't help him any, or make him better. He hoped he would get off—go somewhere, where they couldn't find him, and stay there.

He wondered where he was, and if he had money enough to see him through. He might be no good—he sure wasn't!—but he was Jessie's brother, and Jessie believed in him and thought a lot of him. It would be hard lines for that little girl if Harry were caught. Bill Brown, the meddlesome old freak!—he didn't blame Jessie for not wanting to stop there that night. She did just the right thing.

With all this going round and round, monotonously persistent in his brain, and with the care of four thousand lean kine and more than a hundred saddle-horses—to say nothing of a dozen overworked, fretful cow-punchers—Rowdy acquired the "corrugated brow" fast enough without any cultivation.

The men were as the Silent One had predicted. They made drives that lasted far into the night, stood guard, and got along with so little sleep that it was scarce worth mention, and did many things that shaved close the impossible—just because Rowdy looked at them straightly, with half-closed lids, and asked them if they thought they could.

Pink began to speak of their new foreman as "Moses"; and when the curious asked him why, told them soberly that Rowdy could "hit a rock with his quirt and start a creek running bank full." When Rowdy heard that, he thought of the miles of weary searching, and wished that it were true.

They had left the home ranch a day's drive behind them, and were going north. Rowdy had denied himself the luxury of riding over to see Jessie, and he was repenting the sacrifice in deep gloom and sincerity, when two men rode into camp and dismounted, as if they had a right. The taller one—with brawn and brain a-plenty, by the look of him—announced that he was the sheriff, and would like to stop overnight.

Rowdy gave him welcome half-heartedly, and questioned him craftily. A sheriff is not a detective, and does not mind giving harmless information; so Rowdy learned that they had traced Conroy thus far, and believed that he was ahead of them and making for Canada. He had dodged them cleverly two or three times, but now they had reason to believe that he was not more than half a day's ride before them. They wanted to know if the outfit had seen any one that day, or sign of any one having passed that way.

Rowdy shook his head.

"I bet it was Harry Conroy driving that little bunch uh horses up the creek, just as we come over the ridge," spoke Pink eagerly.

Rowdy could have choked him. "He wouldn't be driving a lot of horses," he interposed quickly.

"Well, he might," argued Pink. "If I was making a quick get-away, and my horse was about played out—like his was apt t' be—I'd sure round up the first bunch I seen, and catch me a fresh one—if I was a horse-thief. I'll bet yuh—"

The sheriff had put down his cup of coffee. "Is there any place where a man could corral a bunch on the quiet?" he asked crisply. It was evident that Pink's theory had impressed him.

"Yes, there is. There's an old corral up at the ford—Drowning Ford, they call it—that I'd use, if it was me. It was an old line camp, and there's a cabin. It's down on the flat by the creek, and it's as God-forsaken a place as a man'd want t' hide in, or t' change mounts." Pink hitched up his chapbelt and looked across at Rowdy. He was aching for a sight of Harry Conroy in handcuffs, and he was certain that Rowdy felt the same. "If it was me," he added speculatively, "and I thought I was far enough in the lead, I'd stop there till morning."

"How far is it from here?" demanded the sheriff, standing up.

Pink told him he guessed it was five miles. Whereupon the sheriff announced his intention of going up there at once, and Pink hinted rather strongly that he would like to go with them. The sheriff did not know Pink; he looked down at his slimness and at the yellow fringe of curls showing under his hat brim, at his pink cheeks and dimples and girlish hands, and threw back his head in a loud ha! ha!

Pink asked him politely, but rather stiffly, what there was funny about it. The sheriff laughed louder and longer; then, being the sort of man who likes a joke now and then, even in the way of business, he solemnly deputized Pink, and patted him on the shoulder and told him gravely that they couldn't possibly do without him.

It looked for a minute as if Pink were going at him with his fists—but he didn't. He reflected that one must not offer violence to an officer of the law, and that, being made a deputy, he would have to go, anyway; so he gritted his teeth and buckled on his gun, and went along sulkily.

They rode silently, for the most part, and swiftly.

Even in the dusk they could see where a band of horses had been driven at a gallop along the creek bank. When they neared the place it was dark. Pink pulled up and spoke for the first time since leaving the tent.

"We better tie up our horses here and walk," he said, quite unconscious of the fact that he was usurping the leadership, and thinking only of their quest.

But the sheriff was old at the business, and not too jealous of his position. He signed to his deputy proper, and they dismounted.

When they started on, Pink was ahead. The sheriff observed that Pink's gun still swung in its scabbard at his hip, and he grinned—but that was because he didn't know Pink. That the gun swung at his hip would have been quite enough for any one who did know him; it didn't take Pink all day to get into action.

Ten rods from the corral, which they could distinguish as a black blotch in the sparse willow growth, Pink turned and stopped them. "I know the layout here," he whispered. "I'll just sneak ahead and rubber around. You Rubes sound like the beginning of a stampede, in this brush."

The sheriff had never before been called a Rube—to his face, at least. The audacity took his breath; and when he opened his mouth for scathing speech, Pink was not there. He had slipped away, like a slim, elusive shadow, and the sheriff did not even know the exact direction of his going. There was nothing for it but to wait.

In five minutes Pink appeared with a silent suddenness that startled them more than they would like to own.

"He's somewheres around," he announced, in a murmur that would not carry ten feet. "He's got a horse in the corral, and, from the sound, he's got him all saddled; and the gate's tied shut with a rope."

"How d'yuh know?" grunted the sheriff crossly.

"Felt of it, yuh chump. He's turned the bunch loose and kept up a fresh one, like I said he would. It's blame dark, but I could see the horse—a big white devil. It's him yuh hear makin' all that racket. If he gits away now—"

"Well, we didn't come for a chin-whackin' bee," snapped the sheriff. "I come out here t' git him."

Pink gritted his teeth again, and wished the sheriff was just a man, so he could lick him. He led them forward without a word, thinking that Rowdy wanted Harry Conroy captured.

The sheriff circled warily the corral, peered through the rails at the great white horse that ran here and there, whinnying occasionally for the band, and heard the creak of leather and the rattle of the bit. Pink was right; the horse was saddled, ready for immediate flight.

"Maybe he's in the cabin," he whispered, coming up where Pink stood listening tensely at all the little night sounds. Pink turned and crept silently to the right, keeping in the deepest shade, while the others followed willingly. They were beginning to see the great advantage of having Pink along, even if he had called them Rubes.

The cabin door yawned wide open, and creaked weirdly as the light wind moved it; the interior was black and silent—suspiciously silent, in the opinion of the sheriff. He waited for some time before venturing in, fearing an ambush. Then he caught the flicker of a shielded match, called out to Conroy to surrender, and leveled his gun at the place.

There was no answer but the faint shuffle of stealthy feet on the board floor. The sheriff called another warning, cocked his gun—and came near shooting Pink, who walked composedly out of the door into the sheriff's astonished face. The sheriff had been sure that Pink was just behind him.

"What the hell," began the sheriff explosively.

"He ain't here," said Pink simply. "I crawled in the window and hunted the place over."

The sheriff glared at him dumbly; he could not reconcile Pink's daredevil behavior with Pink's innocent, girlish appearance.

"I tell yuh the corral's what we want t' keep cases on," Pink added insistently. "He's sure somewheres around—I'd gamble on it. He saddled that horse t' git away on. That horse is sure the key t' this situation, old-timer. If you fellows'll keep cases on the gate, I'll cover the rear."

He made his way quietly to the back of the corral, inwardly much amused at the tractability of the sheriff, who took his deputy obediently to watch the gate.

Pink squatted comfortably in the shade of a willow and wished he dared indulge in a cigarette, and wondered what scheme Harry was trying to play.

Fifty feet away the big white horse still circled round and round, rattling his bridle impatiently and shaking the saddle in an occasional access of rage, and whinnying lonesomely out into the gloom.

So they waited and waited, and peered into the shadows, and listened to the trampling horse fretting for freedom and his mates.

The cook had just called breakfast when Pink dashed up to the tent, flung himself from his horse, and confronted Rowdy—a hollow-eyed, haggard Rowdy who had not slept all night, and whose eyes questioned anxiously.

"Well," Rowdy said, with what passed for composure, "did you get him?"

Pink leaned against his horse, with one hand reaching up and gripping tightly the horn of the saddle. His cheeks held not a trace of color, and his eyes were full of a great horror.

"They're bringin' him t' camp," he answered huskily. "We found a horse—a big white horse they call the Fern Outlaw"—the Silent One started and came closer, listening intently; evidently he knew the horse—"saddled in the corral, and the gate tied shut. We dubbed around a while, but we didn't find—Harry. So we camped down by the corral and waited. We set there all night—and the horse faunching around inside something fierce. When—it come daybreak—I seen something—by the fence, inside. It was—Harry." Pink shivered and moistened his dry lips. "That Fern Outlaw—some uh the boys know—is a devil t' mount. He'd got Harry down—hell, Rowdy! it—it was sure—awful. He'd been there all night—and that horse stomping."

"Shut up!" Rowdy turned all at once deathly sick. He had once seen a man who had been trampled by a maddened, man-killing horse. It had not been a pretty sight. He sat down weakly and covered his face with his shaking hands.

The others stood around horrified, muttering disjointed, shocked sentences.

Pink lifted his head from where it had fallen upon his arm. "One thing, Rowdy—I done. You can tell Jessie. I shot that horse."

Rowdy dropped his hands and stood up. Yes, he must tell Jessie.

"You'll have to take the herd on," he told Pink in his masterful way. "I'll catch you to-morrow some time. I've got to go back and tell Jessie. You know the trail I was going to take—straight across to Wild Horse Lake. From there you strike across to North Fork—and if I don't overtake you on the way, I'll hit camp some time in the night. It's all plain sailing."

CHAPTER 13.
Rowdy Finds Happiness.

Miss Conroy was rather listlessly endeavoring to persuade the First Reader class that "catch" should not be pronounced "ketch," when she saw Rowdy ride past the window. Intuition of something amiss sent her to the door before he reached it.

"Can't you give the kids a day off?" he began, without preface. "I've got such a lot to talk about—and I don't come very often." He thought that his tone was perfectly natural; but all the same she turned white. He rode on to a little tree and tied his horse—not that it was necessary to tie him, but to avoid questions.

Miss Conroy went in and dismissed the children, although it was only fifteen minutes after nine. They gathered up their lunch-pails and straggled out reluctantly, round-eyed, and curious. Rowdy waited until the last one had gone before he went in. Miss Conroy sat in her chair on the platform, and she was still white; otherwise she seemed to have herself well in hand.

"It's about Harry," she asserted, rather sharply.

"Have they—caught him?"

Rowdy stopped half-way down the aisle and stared. "How did you know they were—after him?"

"He came to me night before last, and—told me." She bit her lip, took firm hold on her honesty and her courage, and went on steadily. "He came because he—wanted money. I've wanted to see you since, to tell you that— I misjudged you. I know all about your—trouble, and I want you to know that I think you are—that you did quite right. You are to understand that I cannot honestly uphold—Harry. He is—not the kind of brother—I thought."

Rowdy went clanking forward till only the table stood between. "Did he tell you?" he demanded, in a curious, breathless fashion.

"No, he did not. He denied everything. It was Pink. He told me long ago— that evening, just after you—the last time I saw you. I told him he—lied. I tried not to believe it, but I did. Pink knew I would; he said so. The other night I asked Harry about—those things he did to you. He lied to me. I'd have forgiven him—but he lied. I—can't forgive that. I—"

"Hush!" Rowdy threw out a gloved hand quickly. He could not bear to let her go on like that.

She looked up at him, and all at once she was shaking. "There's something— tell me!"

"They didn't take him," he said slowly, weighing each word and looking down at her pityingly "They never will. He—had an accident. A horse—fell with him—and—he was dead when they picked him up." It was as merciful a version as he could make it, but the words choked him, even then. "Girlie!" He went around and knelt, with his arms holding her close.

After a long while he spoke again, smoothing her hair absently, and never noticing that he had not taken off his gloves. His gray hat was pushed aslant as his head rested against hers.

"Perhaps, girlie, it's for the best. We couldn't have saved him from—the other; and that would have been worse, don't you think? We'll forget all but the good in him"—he could not help thinking that there would not be much to remember—"and I'll get a little home ready, and come back and get you before snow flies—and—you'll be kind of happy, won't you?

"Maybe you haven't heard—but Eagle Creek has made me foreman of his outfit that's going to Canada. It's a good position. I can make you comfortable, girlie—and happy. Anyway, I'll try, mighty hard. You'll be ready for me when I come—won't you, girlie?"

Miss Conroy raised her face, all tear-stained, but, with the light of happiness fighting the sorrow in her eyes, nodded just enough to make the movement perceptible, and settled her head to a more comfortable nestling-place on his shoulder.